## About The Book

THIS exciting novel is set in the American southwest after the Civil War. A young Navajo boy, sold into slavery in New Mexico, dreams of nothing but returning to his home canyon and family. For four long years he must live with this dream while he does back-breaking labor on a New Mexican hacienda. His loneliness is made bearable by a relation of friendship with the owner's son, Tomás, and a grudging regard for the white overseer, Jake.

The story teems with adventure, drama, horses, subplots, and complex human relationships. The interweaving of these elements and the boy's disillusionment upon his escape and return home, result in an absorbing and deeply touching reading experience which reinforces social and moral values and underlines the resiliency of the human spirit.

# NAVAJO SLAVE

## by Lynne Gessner

HARVEY HOUSE, PUBLISHERS
New York, New York

Dedicated to my beloved grandson,
Johnathan Robert Doyle

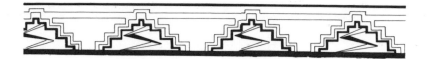

# The Raid

GASPING as the icy wind hit his muscular body, Straight Arrow raced across the new fallen snow, clad only in moccasins and breechclout. His black hair was gathered in a big *chonga* knot at his neck, and around his throat hung a single blue turquoise stone on a leather thong. He headed toward Spider Rock, a red stone column half a mile away that rose hundreds of feet from the canyon floor. Around him the red walls towered, their tops disappearing into storm clouds that hung low.

He shivered, not only from the cold but from a nameless dread. His father had not returned last night, and although it was not unusual for a great Navajo warrior like Red Band to be gone longer than expected, something warned Straight Arrow that this time it meant trouble.

He wanted to go back to the hogan and tell his family to make ready to hide, but his years of training kept his feet moving toward Spider Rock. For over five years—ever since he was six summers old—he had been made to rise at dawn and run to Spider Rock and back, wearing only his breechclout, no matter whether summer or winter. And once back at the hogan, he would have to plunge into

7

the shallow water of Tsegi River. This was to give him strength and endurance.

More than anything else in the world, Straight Arrow wanted to be a warrior like his father. Red Band was fearless, strong, and wise. He was highly feared by the hated Ute Indians, by the sly Mexicans, and by the clever white soldiers of Colonel Kit Carson. In all Straight Arrow's eleven years of life, he could never remember his father showing the slightest fear. Although to his family he was a man of gentleness and understanding, to his enemies Red Band was a merciless foe.

Eagerly Straight Arrow looked forward to this summer when he would be twelve, for then he would be ready to go on important raids with his father.

As Straight Arrow's body warmed from the exercise, he glanced across his canyon and felt a deep love for it. The fresh snow made powdery piles on rocks and stumps and clung like bits of wool to the bare cottonwood trees. There was a silence in this canyon—the silence of the long-dead, the Ancient Ones—and of the families who now lived within its towering walls, people who had learned to live at peace with their land. No wonder it was sacred to the Navajos—it was so grand and so massive that even the gods chose to dwell there.

"Our world is beautiful," Straight Arrow thought, his round black eyes shining with delight. "There is no place on earth to compare with our sacred Tsegi Canyon."

He reached Spider Rock and raced around the talus slope at the base. With chest heaving from the exertion and lungs burning from the biting air, he longed to rest, but he dared not. Red Band, although a kind father, was a stern teacher. He allowed no resting.

"How can you be strong and endure, if you must always rest?" he would demand whenever Straight Arrow complained. Even more than he feared his father's wrath, he was terrified of Spider Woman who lived atop Spider Rock and watched all Navajo children. It was said that when children disobeyed their parents, she came down from her perch and dragged them back up, where she would eat them. Straight Arrow had never seen her or known anyone she had stolen, but he could see the top of the stone column, white with what his mother, Slender Woman, said were the bleaching bones of children.

So he did not slow his pounding feet, but continued around the red column, glancing fearfully up to the top. Fervently he hoped she would see that he was being obedient. From behind him he heard a drumming noise and spun around in sudden fear.

With profound relief he recognized his father coming around the bend on his horse. He was riding fast and his strong square face showed deep concern. His powerful shoulders were hunched forward against the cold, and strands of his long black hair had come loose from the *chonga* knot on his neck and from the red headband that had given him his name. Despite the cold, the horse was lathered.

"My father," Straight Arrow called out anxiously, remembering his earlier feeling of trouble afoot.

Without slowing, Red Band headed toward his son. "Get up behind," he called and, with a fluid movement,

Straight Arrow vaulted up behind him and clung to his muscular body. Rigid training had taught him to obey instantly, although he could not understand why his father would relieve him of the long run back to the hogan.

"The soldiers—that white enemy, Kit Carson—they have burned the hogan of Brown Shirt," Red Band said in a voice cold with anger and indignation. "They have killed two of his sons."

Stunned by such news, Straight Arrow could not speak and he shivered as the cold wind whipped his sweating naked body. Brown Shirt lived near the mouth of Tsegi Canyon, which meant the enemy was now *in* the canyon.

Straight Arrow dared not shame his father by showing the stab of fear that had come to him at his father's statement, so he forced his voice to sound normal. "What must we do?"

"We must leave at once!"

"Leave?" The word was wrenched out of Straight Arrow because he could not imagine leaving their sacred land.

"We will ride to the small ravine where we usually hide," Red Band explained. "At our first chance we will flee—but only for a while." Straight Arrow felt the strong back stiffen as his father's head rose proudly. "No matter where we are driven, we will return to this canyon. Remember that, my son, remember it well. No one can take it from the Navajo!"

Pride in his father and in his race made Straight Arrow's chest swell. Were they not the *Dineh*—The People! This was where they belonged.

They passed the cornfield, the peach orchard, and the

sheep corral where the black dog waited while New Found Boy opened the gate. He was a Ute boy, the same age as Straight Arrow.

"Leave the sheep in the pen, my son," Red Band called out. "We must leave quickly. Get the horses."

New Found Boy's placid round face mirrored dismay, and Straight Arrow knew that this boy, raised as brother to himself and his small sister, Timid One, would find it hard to leave his beloved flock behind. Unlike Straight Arrow, he had no desire to be a warrior, because at heart he was a sheepherder. But his love for Red Band bade him obey, though he glanced longingly at the woolly creatures as he headed for the horses in another corral.

At the sound of their voices, Slender Woman and Timid One came out of the round mud and log hogan, followed by Grandfather.

"Mount your horses," Red Band ordered as they neared him. "The soldiers come."

"We will need food," Slender Woman exclaimed and started back to the hogan, clutching her blanket around her body, now heavy with a child in her womb.

"No! There is no time. The soldiers bring death."

"Come, little one," Grandfather said to Timid One and lifted her onto one of the horses as New Found Boy turned them out of the corral.

Straight Arrow looked approvingly at the wrinkled old man. Although he was no longer a warrior who went on raids, he sensed the danger and acted without question. In his own time he had faced perils greater than this, and the telling of these stories around the campfire had made

Straight Arrow yearn even more for the time when he, too, would be a noted fighter like his father and grandfather.

Straight Arrow slid off Red Band's horse and darted into the hogan for his buckskin shirt and his blanket, then gathered his bow and arrows, racing out to his horse and straddling its bare back in one easy leap.

"Just a few sheep?" New Found Boy begged plaintively.

"No. We must go without food, without sheep—even without the dog." Red Band's voice was harsh and urgent.

They rode out single file, clutching their blankets around them so only their eyes showed. The white soldiers had come into the canyon several times during the summer to steal horses and to threaten the Navajos. Red Band's family then had merely fled to the small ravine—a short ride down the canyon—to hide their sheep, horses, and themselves until the soldiers grew tired of harrassing the Indians and left the canyon. Yet today Red Band would not take so much as one sheep. And the burning of Brown Shirt's hogan and the killing of his sons—that was something new and threatening.

They raced past Spider Rock. At this point another large canyon opened to the east, but they went on not turning. Cold blasts of wind tugged at their blankets and Straight Arrow shivered, wishing they had something to eat. But Slender Woman had wanted to wait until Red Band returned from his scouting trip before serving their morning meal, and now there was no time.

They rounded a bend and Red Band raised his hand for silence. In the distance they heard the dull drumming of hoofbeats in sand—the white soldiers. From the sound there were many!

"We cannot make it to the ravine!" Red Band said, his voice low and tense. He wheeled his horse around. "Come—quickly. We go deeper into the canyon."

"I am afraid," Timid One wailed, her round face peering out from her blanket in terror.

"Foolish one," Red Band teased, pausing long enough to pat her shoulder reassuringly. "We will hide you in the farthest corner where not even the blue jay will find you."

Straight Arrow knew the teasing of his father was to hide his embarrassment at having a child who would express fear. Sometimes during his own severe training, Straight Arrow had been frightened, but never had he dared let his fear show. To do so would have disgraced his father. He was ashamed now to remember how he had often complained about Red Band's unyielding and often almost cruel discipline and his demand for immediate and complete obedience. Today he saw that this training had been for just such a time as this when they would have to use all their cunning to survive.

"Ride fast," Red Band urged, prodding them along. "If they see us, they will kill."

Once again Spider Rock rose into view and beyond it, by the junction of the two canyons, was their hogan.

"Go into the south canyon and ride in the riverbed so you leave no trail," Red Band ordered as they came to the familiar grounds. "Ride fast." To Grandfather he said, "Take them to the small box canyon by the bent tree. Hide them well. And you, my son," he said to New

Found Boy, who was shivering from the cold, "protect your sister. Do not let her cry." To them all he added, "Remember, you must make no sound. Keep the horses quiet. And take mine with you."

"What will *you* do, my father?" Straight Arrow asked.

Red Band nodded his head toward the high mesa that rose between the southern and eastern canyons. It was a place Straight Arrow had often gone to, a vantage point where he could look down on his home. "I will go up on the ridge and shoot arrows. They will seem to come from the east canyon so the soldiers will seek us in there and not this canyon."

Proud of his father, Straight Arrow smiled in approval. It was just such cleverness that enabled the Navajos to resist the white man. In fact, it was the cunning of the Navajo that so infuriated this Colonel Kit Carson that he was determined to make prisoners of them all.

"My father, let me go with you," he begged. "Two of us shooting arrows might make them think there are many in the other canyon." He pulled his tense young body up as tall as he could so Red Band would see he was ready to fight in a real battle. He sensed that this moment was a testing time—whether he was now considered a man.

Red Band hesitated, studying him. "Come," he ordered finally.

Elated, Straight Arrow followed his father, racing on foot back to the sheep corral while the family rode deeper into the southern canyon, taking the two extra horses with them.

"First, drive a few sheep into the east canyon—quickly!" his father ordered.

Straight Arrow released ten sheep, then ordered the dog to drive them into the east canyon. Obediently it trotted off, nipping at the heels of the sheep.

"Now we go to the ridge. Cover our trail," Red Band said. As they raced to the steep stone wall, they both threw fresh snow over their footprints.

Leaning against the redstone wall was a crude ladder made of saplings lashed together with deerskin thongs. Red Band climbed first, with Straight Arrow nimbly following. On a narrow ledge where the ladder ended, they paused and pulled up the ladder to hide it. Then they used toeholds carved in the stone to reach the top.

Hurrying out to the point, they saw nearly twenty soldiers milling around below them.

"We had little time to spare!" Straight Arrow was shocked at how close the soldiers had been behind them. Worriedly he wondered whether the family was now safely hidden and whether he and his father had covered their tracks well enough. He could see their hogan, the peach orchard, the cornfields, and the sheep corral.

Eagerly Straight Arrow looked at the soldiers. This was his first real battle and he was anxious to be doing something. Pulling an arrow from his quiver, he turned to walk to the far ridge.

"No—no, it is not time yet," Red Band warned him. "Learn patience, my son." He shook his head in concern. "If you would be a warrior, do not act hastily. See, they are not yet ready to search for us. To shoot an arrow now would be unwise. We will wait."

Flushing, Straight Arrow pulled his blanket tight against the stinging cold wind and waited. Would he ever learn? Always his father had to remind him of things he had already been taught.

Almost immediately his embarrassment was replaced by fury and indignation as he watched the soldiers below. Slowly and deliberately they rode back and forth over the snow-covered cornfield, the horses' hoofs destroying every root and seed. He groaned inwardly as the ring of their axes echoed on the sheer stone walls and one by one the beautiful, snow-trimmed peach trees toppled to the ground.

"Our peaches!" he started to say mournfully then bit his lip to keep back the words. A warrior could not show despair, not even if his favorite peach trees were gone forever.

When the soldiers began to slaughter the sheep, however, firing wantonly into the corral, he could not hide his misery. He ground his teeth together in fury. "I would rather die than live in captivity! Who are they that they think they can defeat us—*The People*!" His lean dark face hardened. "We will never be defeated." His voice caught in his throat. "Never!"

Red Band touched his shoulder. "You speak the truth, my son. To live in captivity is not the Navajo way. So, for now, we hide."

"My father—look! Our hogan. . . ."

The soldiers, their work finished, had finally put a torch

to the house and were warming themselves in its blaze. Until now, Straight Arrow had felt only contempt for the white man. But from this moment, he vowed he would truly be a warrior like his father, a killer of soldiers, and he would never surrender to these pale-faced men.

Down below the soldiers mounted and began searching for signs that would show where the occupants of the hogan had gone. Straight Arrow curled his lip in disdain. These stupid men, with their carelessness, had covered all sign of trail. Then he saw that they had spotted the tracks of the ten sheep being driven into the east canyon.

Beside him, his father spoke in a voice as cold as the icy wind. "It is time."

Together they took arrows from their quivers. "There must be no doubt that the arrows came from the east canyon," Red Band said. "They must think we have gone there, taking some sheep with us."

They leaned out at the farthermost point and, as fast as they could, loosed two arrows apiece from their bows, then dropped back behind the bushes. The squeal of a wounded horse and the scream of a man told them that the arrows had found their mark.

Straight Arrow parted the bushes and looked down. "They go where we want them to go," he whispered with satisfaction.

"Come," said Red Band as he slithered back from the edge. "Quickly, now."

They climbed down the steep walls. Once on the canyon floor they hid the ladder, then raced through the snow to the little box canyon where the family was hiding.

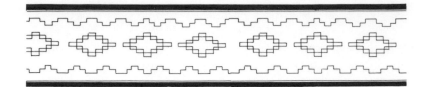

# Capture

ONCE in the rock-choked canyon, Straight Arrow looked around. At first he could see no one; then slowly, as the family realized it was not soldiers who had entered, they came out of hiding from behind huge boulders and from inside small dark caves covered by brush. All but Timid One.

Swollen with the importance of his new stature as a fighter, Straight Arrow demanded, "Where is our sister?"

Grandfather, wrinkled but fiercely erect, grinned mischievously. With a jutting of his chin he pointed to a dense growth of thorny cats-claw and creosote bush. Straight Arrow peered into the shadows, yet saw nothing. Then slowly the child stood up, two round dark eyes staring seriously at him.

Red Band chuckled as he reached over the brambles and lifted her out. "Surely not even the jaybird could have found you." He hugged her and put her down, his face once more tense as he told them what he had seen done to their home.

"Now we must hurry and leave the canyon," Grandfather suggested, the fire of battle in his eyes.

Red Band shook his head. "I must see first if there are more soldiers. And there are Utes in the canyon. I had to use cunning to avoid them when coming back this morning. They are supposed to help the white soldiers find us, but they sell their captives to the slave traders."

At the mention of the slave traders, Straight Arrow remembered his uncle, Tale Teller. Years before Straight Arrow's birth, a Ute had captured this uncle and sold him to the Mexicans as a slave. Straight Arrow remembered the day he had returned after sixteen years in the silver mines—a quiet, frail shadow of a man who had told tales of incredible horror. It was thus that the family had learned the language of the Mexicans, both to hear and speak, because Tale Teller after his return spoke more easily in the foreign tongue than in his own. It was only this summer that he died.

"We cannot stay here too long," Slender Woman said, drawing farther into her blanket. Her face, though tight from hunger and weariness, held its usual gentle patience so familiar to Straight Arrow. "Without food our bodies will not be able to fight the cold."

From under his blanket, New Found Boy pulled out a bunch of roots. "I found them where I was hiding," he explained simply, and handed them to Slender Woman and his sister. "Take them. I am not yet hungry and I shall find more."

With affection—touched by a trace of gentle scorn— Straight Arrow looked at his brother. New Found Boy found no excitement in raiding, and with his sensitive face and sympathetic eyes, he appeared too mild of manner to ever be a warrior. Yet Straight Arrow felt that in his quietness there was strength. No wonder Red Band loved him.

"Our home and our sheep are gone," Timid One said plaintively, leaning against her mother while she gnawed on a root. "Soon this food will be gone." She fingered a piece of turquoise dangling on a leather cord around her neck. "All any of us have left is our turquoise. And what good will that do? We can't eat it." She rubbed a fist in her eye.

"The turquoise will keep away evil spirits, daughter of no courage," Slender Woman chided her.

"But suppose the soldiers capture us. They'll take our turquoise and then we won't have *anything*!"

"The child speaks truth," Red Band said. "I will hide it." He held out his hands to the group as they stood huddled behind a large red rock for protection from the wind. The clouds were still black overhead and Straight Arrow longed for the warmth of the sun as he removed the silver concho belt from his waist and the bead from around his neck. One by one they handed him their prized jewelry—silver and turquoise belts, bracelets inlaid with the blue stone, and Slender Woman's necklace of turquoise nuggets, almost all of it made by Grandfather's nimble fingers. "We shall not let them take our turquoise," Red Band said. "We will need it to buy more sheep when they are gone." Carefully he wrapped the jewelry in a piece of sheepskin.

Slender Woman looked longingly at the bundle. "Do not hide it far away," she begged softly. "We need the protection the turquoise gives us."

Red Band nodded and pulled his blanket tighter around his shoulders. "I will search for food while I am gone."

Straight Arrow saw the familiar gleam come to his father's eyes. This was what Red Band liked—a challenge—how to find food in this frozen land filled with soldiers and prowling Utes. Perhaps he would even steal it from the soldiers themselves. Although the white man thought stealing was wrong, to Red Band's people it was a skill. Any man who could sneak into a forbidden place and take what he needed without being caught was highly regarded.

"My father," Straight Arrow said eagerly, "while we watched the soldiers I saw one horse carrying food boxes. They must plan to make a camp farther in the east canyon. We could sneak close to them and take the food."

Red Band smiled in approval. "Well done, my son. You have observed carefully as I taught you. Very well, we shall take their food. Come." To the others he gave one final warning. "Keep yourselves hidden. Do not leave this canyon!" Then with a brief smile that eased the tension on his face he added, "We shall come back."

Feeling very important, Straight Arrow followed his father and they set out at once, traveling swiftly and silently on foot, hugging the canyon wall and keeping in the deep shadows of the overhanging sandstone cliffs. At Spider Rock they paused where the talus at the base sloped upward to the red stone finger pointing to the cloudy sky.

"We will bury our turquoise here," Red Band said. "The soldiers will never climb up to search, and if the waters of the river should rise before we can come for the stones, it will be safe." They studied the area leading into both canyons, but there was no sign of soldiers or Ute Indians. Quickly they climbed the rocky slope to the top of the talus heap. Using a stick, Red Band dug a deep hole and buried the sheepskin-wrapped bundle, then he scattered the gravel over it before standing up. "Now our turquoise is safe. Your mother will feel better, knowing it is not far away." He smiled. "See, the turquoise guards our home ground. Someday we will rebuild our hogan and the turquoise will help us. We will not be poor, as the white man wants us to be." Then he raised his eyes to the top of the slender stone column. "Oh, Spider Woman, guardian of the Navajo, protect our stones, protect our homes, and protect my family," he prayed softly. Then he squared his shoulders and they both scrambled down the slope.

Straight Arrow glanced wistfully at the mouth of the southern canyon, where their charred hogan stood like some evil spirit gazing at them. He eyed the bloody mass in the corral. There was much meat there, but the soldiers had ridden their horses over the dead animals, spoiling the flesh.

They headed into the eastern canyon and soon saw the bloody remains of the rest of their herd. A bullet had ended the little black dog's efforts to defend his sheep. They followed the trail of the soldiers and, after many bends and turns in the canyon, they heard voices. Leaving the walls, Red Band and his son moved carefully from bush to bush.

When they finally neared the soldiers, Straight Arrow saw a roaring fire in the center of their camp. What a waste of wood, he thought. No Navajo would do such a thing. For one weak moment he longed to warm himself at those leaping flames, then he pulled himself up. Whining about the cold was not the Navajo way.

Red Band leaned close to him. "Listen carefully, my son," he whispered. "Those boxes are unguarded now, probably because they have eaten. I shall go over by those rocks." He indicated a cluster of boulders some distance from the camp. "From there I will shoot an arrow, then roll down a stone. That will bring the soldiers in my direction. You know what to do."

"Yes. But how will you get away?"

Red Band turned his head to a grove of big bare cottonwoods near the boulders. "I will go that way and find a place to hide until dark, then I will make my way back to you. Don't take too much food or it will slow you down." He put a hand on his son's shoulder, his eyes proud. "Be careful, my son. But you well know how to raid and how to get away."

Though outwardly Straight Arrow tried to appear casual at his father's rare praise, inwardly he was bursting with joy. At last he was participating in a real raid and his father considered him capable. He longed to say that being a warrior like Red Band was his greatest ambition, but such was not the Navajo way, and his brown face remained expressionless.

Red Band melted into the shadows and Straight Arrow began to inch his way closer to the bushes beside the food boxes. He stopped and waited.

Soon he heard a shriek of pain and saw one of the soldiers tug at an arrow imbedded in his arm. At the same moment, when a small stone clattered down from the top of the rocks, the soldiers grabbed their guns and began running toward the sound.

Keeping the food boxes between himself and the soldiers, Straight Arrow darted forward. Then he paused and tossed a piece of wood out beyond the wounded soldier still in camp. Startled, the man spun around and in that moment Straight Arrow reached the boxes. One was locked and he peered into the other. He couldn't believe what he saw! Instead of much food, there were only sacks and pots and empty tins. There was nothing to take but a few small shriveled apples.

He grabbed them and stuffed them into the fold of his blanket. Then silently as a shadow, he disappeared into the bushes and headed away. When he heard gunfire, he looked back, but saw no sign of his father, so he ran until he reached a place near the wall where he could see the grove of cottonwoods.

As he looked toward the big trees, the figure of Red Band appeared and almost immediately a volley of gunfire echoed down the canyon. Straight Arrow saw his father pause as a wailing cry escaped his lips; then he fell face down into the snow and was still.

Straight Arrow stood rooted to the ground staring at the fallen figure in the distance. It couldn't be true—not Red

Band! But the figure did not move and the canyon—the whole world to Straight Arrow—suddenly seemed like a big draining void. He felt as if he were in some deep well of blackness with no bottom to it. Desperately—though there was no one to see—he fought to hide his emotion. He could not disgrace Red Band's final moment of life by expressing grief.

He had never considered the possibility that his father could die—not even today when he had bravely faced such odds in order that his family might have food. He knew now that such a thought had never occurred to him because his father had not shown fear. Remembering this, he realized that Red Band had died as heroically as he had lived—a warrior any son could be proud of. And Straight Arrow's head rose proudly. Now he was the fighter in the family. He would show his father he had learned his lessons well.

He heard a faint sound and instinctively made an effort to move on, but the loss of his father was still too heavy, and he looked back once more, hoping wildly that the familiar figure would get up and flee.

Without warning a rough hand slapped across his mouth and strong arms held him tightly. The few apples spilled to the ground and Straight Arrow looked up to see a gloating Indian face above him. Too late he realized that he had allowed his grief to make him careless. How else could he have fallen prisoner to a despised Ute!

# The Slave Trail

FOR TWO DAYS Straight Arrow traveled with the Ute Indian, his arms tightly bound. Although he was wrapped in his blanket, he suffered greatly from the cold, but it was as nothing to the misery in his heart. On their way out of the canyon he had seen burned hogans and trampled cornfields. He had also seen many dead Navajo warriors who in life had been brave men, but who in death were *chindi*—contaminated by evil spirits. Straight Arrow kept as far from them as he possibly could.

Thinking about the *chindi*, he remembered with sinking heart that he had no turquoise with him. Without the sacred blue stone, he was like a bow without an arrow—useless. Struggle as he would to get free, there was no way he could escape.

Late on the second day the Ute sold him to a slave trader—a fat Mexican named Manuel. After untying Straight Arrow's arms, the Mexican tied a rope around his neck and shoved him into a big wagon filled with other Indians—all as miserable as he was. He pulled his knees up under his chin and wrapped his blanket around him so that only his eyes were exposed. It was a fine blanket—heavy and warm—and made for him by Slender Woman. He knew he would have to guard it well or it would be stolen.

The thick rope around his neck felt like a circle of cactus thorns. From time to time he clawed at it desperately, but there was no way he could free himself from it. It was too thick to chew, and anyway, there was not enough give in it to enable him to raise it to his mouth.

A girl beside him with a broken front tooth spoke in Navajo. "It will be worse in a day or so," she said, pulling aside a flap of her blanket. The rope around her neck was red with blood—dark where it had dried and bright where the blood was new—and underneath there was a chafed, raw welt. He ground his teeth in rage. Never would he sink so low as these, where he would accept defeat as inevitable. He was a fighter and he would never forget it.

The journey from the land of the Navajo to the land of the haciendas of New Mexico was a wretched nightmare of cold days in the wagon and freezing nights huddled together with the others under whatever shelter was available. Each evening Manuel cooked and ate his meat and beans with gusto. But the captive Indians were forced to grub in the frozen earth for whatever scant food they could find—nuts, roots, cactus fruit, and seeds.

The days of misery gave Straight Arrow many occasions to remember his father's stern lessons in survival. Whenever Red Band had taken him on a raid or even on a training ride, he first had to find his own food—enough to sustain him for a day—before Red Band would share the meat he carried with him.

And how many times he'd complained—especially when he was given no water all day in the hot summer—or when he was made to bathe in the river of Tsegi during the winter! He longed to tell his father that now he understood—now he was grateful for the training. He was stronger than any of the others and he'd been able to find more food.

One mid-afternoon they reached an area of many houses. In spite of the hunger pains in his stomach and the aching misery of his neck, Straight Arrow stared about him in amazement. He had been to the Pueblo villages of the Zuni Indians when he had gone on raids with his father, but never had he seen anything like this. The streets were full of people—white soldiers and cowboys, ladies in bright dresses, and men on spirited horses with shining saddles decorated with silver. There were carts and mules and dogs and sheep. And houses—more than he had ever seen in his whole life—some of them hardly bigger than the humblest hogan, but others—well, he knew nothing fine enough to compare them with. The noise and bustle confused him, bringing home more clearly how far he was from the quiet solitude of his beloved canyon.

Manuel shouted suddenly and the wagon halted. "*Hola*, Don Armando! over here. . . . "

A handsome well-dressed man looked with distaste at Manuel as he walked toward the wagon, his spurs jingling with every step.

Straight Arrow's glance went briefly over the man, then settled on the boy walking beside him. He had never seen a boy like this one. He didn't even look like any of the other children romping and yelling in the dusty street. He was probably about thirteen, and Straight Arrow wondered if he were some sort of chief, or maybe a chief's son. His black boots shone like pool water in the sun and his dark close-fitting suit was decorated along the sleeves and down the pants with what looked like silver thread. A black hat with a beautiful silver band was pulled low over his eyes. Even more than the clothes that made him look like some gaudy bird, Straight Arrow's attention was drawn by the way the boy strutted—like a prancing pony. He reminded Straight Arrow of a wild black horse his father had tried for two summers to catch. Red Band had used every trick known by the Navajos, but it had always eluded him. It would stand just out of reach, looking back, then with a flick of its tail, it would trot off with the same arrogant, proud air that this boy exhibited.

"I have a fine load of slaves today," Manuel said to Don Armando eagerly when he paused. "There is one boy—he would do well on your hacienda." He grinned with a great show of honesty. "Of course, he is wild—but he is strong—and, anyway, who knows better than Don Armando how to tame the wild ones, eh?"

Don Armando's expression of distaste did not change. "Show me."

Manuel scrambled down from his horse. "It is this one, *señor*—" He pulled Straight Arrow to the ground and carelessly yanked the rope from his raw and aching neck, then he shoved him toward Don Armando. "See for yourself if I have not spoken the truth."

Straight Arrow refused to look up, but he felt Don Armando's eyes on him. The man was very tall and slender as a sapling. His brown boots glistened like those of the boy and there was about him an air of great authority.

"You might as well begin to learn how to choose slaves, Miguel," Don Armando said to the elegant boy beside him. "What do you think of this one?"

Miguel walked slowly around Straight Arrow, eyeing him as he might a horse. Straight Arrow knew how he must appear to this young Spaniard—blood from the chafing dry on his deerskin shirt and crusted on his neck, long black hair falling from the *chonga* knot and straggling over his face, and deerskin pants mud-caked and stiff. But these outward things were not important. Inside he was a Navajo, and his head rose defiantly. Impassively he stared back at Miguel, hiding the contempt he felt. This foolish one would not know how to judge a man.

Like Don Armando, Miguel's features were delicately chiseled, his skin a finer texture and lighter brown than that of the slave trader, Manuel, and his hair was glossy black. His eyes, a golden shade of brown, did not reflect any warmth as they studied Straight Arrow.

Miguel nodded without looking up at Don Armando. "He's a filthy, skinny beggar," he said with a look of repugnance, "but he's got good broad shoulders—strong hands, too. The skin looks healthy under that filth, which probably means he isn't diseased. I'd say he's got stamina." Miguel glanced at Don Armando and nodded. "We'll find a use for him."

Despite his loathing for this arrogant boy, Straight Arrow was forced to admit Miguel was more shrewd and perceptive than he'd first thought.

Don Armando smiled. "Very good. Had your brother looked him over he would have seen only the dirt and the leanness. But you see beneath these unimportant details. I'm proud of you."

Don Armando put out a gloved hand and, grabbing Straight Arrow by the hair, pulled his head back so that his face was raised. For a moment their eyes met, then Straight Arrow jerked his head away and the man laughed.

"You are right," he said to Manuel, sounding pleased. "He is a wild one." He pulled a pouch from his pocket and tossed some coins to the slave trader.

"Walk in front of us," he ordered and, when Straight Arrow did not move, he shoved him roughly. "And don't try to escape or I shall be forced to use this." He touched the gun in his belt.

His pride rebelling at the man's ugly, superior tone of voice, Straight Arrow kept his face as expressionless as it had been for days, but he allowed contempt to fill his mind. He remembered what Tale Teller had said about the people called Mexicans—among them there were those called Dons—and they were almost always Spaniards—who considered the ordinary Mexicans and just about everybody else as inferior people. They were the wealthy ones—the *patróns*, the bosses.

In spite of his misery, Straight Arrow almost laughed
aloud in his contempt. When were shiny boots and
swaggering ways ever the measure of a man! Could these
people survive for days on a few roots and nuts? Could
they endure the torment of the rope without a sound?
Could they sleep on the frozen ground and still live? He
thought not. Surely the warrior who withstood all this
suffering was then truly the man. And he knew as never
before what he was—a Navajo, one of *The People*. They
might beat him, make a slave of him, laugh at him, but
they would never defeat him.

He looked up briefly at the girl with the broken tooth
and wondered what would happen to her. Then, as he
scuffed away in the loose dirt of the street, all his thoughts
were centered on his own plight. It should be easy to get
away from this rich Spaniard with so many people milling
around on the street. Carefully he waited his chance and,
when Don Armando stopped to talk to a friend, Straight
Arrow slipped into a passing group of young Mexican
boys.

"Papá!" came a warning cry from Miguel, and a swift
blow to Straight Arrow's head made him fall to his knees.

"Maybe you don't understand Spanish," Don Armando
said grimly, "but I'll wager you'll understand this—and
this. . . . "

The street boys stood around shouting and laughing and
pointing at him, while Miguel stood apart, his face ashen
at the sight of his father's brutality. "Papá, no!" he cried
out, and grabbed at Don Armando's sleeve.

Humiliation and weakness from lack of food, more than

the force of the blows, made it impossible for Straight Arrow to stay even on his knees and he fell full length on the ground.

"Get up," Don Armando ordered.

Somehow, with the taste of dust bitter in his mouth, Straight Arrow struggled to his feet.

"Now—walk here." Don Armando pointed just in front of him.

Straight Arrow walked, shuffling along weakly with no more thought of escape, but telling himself that there would be other times and other chances. He could wait.

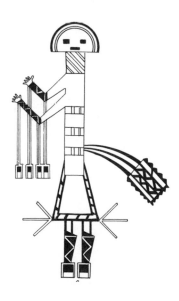

# Don Armando and Miguel

IT WAS almost too great an effort for Straight Arrow to hold his head up while his feet dragged through the dust. Then he smelled the most wonderful odor of cooking food and his mouth watered hungrily. He had eaten nothing at all since the night before last, and not much of anything for days before that.

Don Armando put a heavy hand on his shoulder to stop him, opened the door of a long, low building, and shoved him inside. He stumbled over the sill and fell onto the dirt floor, then crawled into the farthest corner where Don Armando indicated he should wait.

It was a big room, and the voices of many people made a steady droning sound, like the hum of bees. Those big round things on legs were surely what his uncle had called tables. At one of them Don Armando sat down beside another man who greeted him cordially. Miguel sat across from his father, facing Straight Arrow.

"It is good to see you in Santa Fe again, Armando," the friend said to the tall Spaniard. He nodded cordially to Miguel. "And you, Miguel, you look more like Armando every day. Where is Tomás?"

34

"My brother didn't want to come. . . . "

"José, you know Tomás," Don Armando said wearily. "He hates to ride—he hates to look at horses—he hates everything but that music of his. . . . "

"Did you come up for horses then?" José glanced over his shoulder at Straight Arrow. "Or for slaves?"

Don Armando shook his head. "Neither. Miguel and I came up with a load of skins. . . . "

"Are you having any problems down your way with stolen horses?" José asked. "Up here there isn't a range animal to be found and a lot of the cavalry horses seem to disappear. . . . "

"Stolen horses?" Miguel asked with sudden interest. "Really?"

"Yes. I hear there's quite a flourishing business going on in stolen horses between here and Mexico."

"I've had the problem, too," Don Armando replied. "Those thieving Apaches keep raiding my herd. Fortunately I still have quite a few left. And I've managed to get others. But it's a serious problem, José," he said scowling.

"Maybe now that you don't have so many horses, you can get rid of that overseer, Jake. A surly one—that *hombre*. For the life of me, I cannot see why you keep him."

"But no one knows horses like Jake," Miguel said quickly.

Don Armando silenced him with a look. "I keep him because he is useful."

"He hates you," José argued. "Even I could see that the

last time I was there. Listen to your friend, Armando, and get rid of him. I do not trust that one."

"Jake would not bring grief to anyone," Miguel said. "He is too. . . ."

"Bah—he is quarrelsome, but he is a good worker," Don Armando cut in. Then he shrugged and nodded toward Straight Arrow. "Manuel just happened to have this boy—and I just happened to have an extra horse going back—so I bought him. Doesn't look like much, does he? Oh well, he came cheap enough."

In his corner, Straight Arrow crouched, waiting for his meal. It seemed a long time before a young girl brought him a large bowl of beans and a plate of flat round things that looked like the thin corn bread his mother used to fry on a hot stone slab. The girl put the dishes on the floor in front of him and gestured toward the plate, making a scooping motion with her hands. "Tortillas," she said.

He didn't care what they were called. He grabbed one and folded it, using it to spoon the beans into his mouth from the bowl he held beneath his chin. He had taken three mouthfuls in rapid succession, hardly stopping to swallow, when a scalding fire spread through his mouth and his throat. Tears streamed from his eyes and he began to choke. Too late he remembered that he had heard of this fire the Mexicans ate.

Don Armando and the others in the room roared—even Miguel managed a smile—while Straight Arrow wiped his eyes on his sleeve and scowled at the beans. Never had he eaten anything so hot! He would have given his favorite horse for some water.

Looking around wildly, he could not see the girl and
there was no one he dared ask. Miguel raised his hand
and the young girl appeared from behind a door and
hurried over to him, nodding her head as he gave her an
order. Then she scurried away, but in a moment she set a
tin mug of water on the floor beside Straight Arrow.
Greedily he gulped it, cooling his burning mouth. He
began again cautiously, taking small bits of beans and large
pieces of the tortillas. At first he choked every time he
inhaled, but by the time he had finished the beans and
wiped the bowl clean with his last bit of tortilla, he was
breathing almost normally.

When Don Armando finished his meal, he rose and
extended his hand to his friend. "*Adiós*, José. Stay with us
the next time you pass our way. Come, Miguel, we have
much riding before the sun sets."

Pushing Straight Arrow ahead of them, they went out
into the waning light.

"What are you called?" Don Armando asked abruptly
when they had gone a short way.

Straight Arrow decided not to answer. Although he
understood the Spanish he'd heard spoken, as yet he,
himself, had said not a word. For one thing, a Navajo did
not like to tell his name, it was too sacred. Besides, his
fierce Navajo pride prevented him from speaking to this
man he considered inferior.

When he did not answer, Don Armando said impatiently, "All right, since you don't have a name, I'll give
you one—Niño."

Miguel nodded. "It's good enough for him."

Straight Arrow thought that Niño was fine. He knew it meant *boy*, which wasn't really a name at all. But it would do as long as he was with these Spaniards. As Straight Arrow had been the name of his freedom, so Niño would be the name of his captivity.

When they came to the stable, they were greeted by a wizened little Mexican who said, "Ah, Don Armando, and young Miguel, your horses are ready." He led out a big sorrel gelding, a blue roan, and a rangy little dun mare. Attached to the saddle of the gelding was a long coil of rope. The saddle itself was of fine leather with much carving, but the saddle on the blue roan was heavy with silver decorations. Niño decided that Don Armando held the boy, Miguel, in high esteem and saw that he had the best of everything.

Niño ran his hand over the gelding's sleek hide. Like his father, he loved horses and this was as fine a horse as he had ever seen.

"Can you ride without a saddle?" Don Armando asked.

Preoccupied with the horse, he nodded.

"Aha! So you *do* understand Spanish!" Don Armando laughed at the success of his trick. "Well, then get up on the mare."

Grabbing its mane, Niño swung up from the right side, but before he could get a good grip with his legs, the mare bucked and threw him into the dirt. As he shook his head to clear it, he realized that this was no Indian pony. While Don Armando waited and Miguel gave him a look of disdain, he dusted himself off, mounted from the left

and pulled his blanket close about him. It was getting cold
again.

Don Armando flipped the stable man a coin and they
rode out of the city, going south until they reached a
small ranch house. Niño was put into a tiny, windowless
room and given a sheepskin pelt to sleep on before he was
locked in.

As he lay in the blackness, wrapped in Slender
Woman's fine blanket, he realized that for the first time in
many days his body was comfortable. The bruises from
Don Armando's beating and the raw sores on his neck
were as nothing compared to the fact that he was warm,
full, and well-sheltered.

The familiar smell of the sheepskin brought a rush of
memories of his bed in the hogan and of his family, and
homesickness almost overwhelmed him. He wondered
what had happened to his family. Without Red Band, they
could not survive in such cold for long. No doubt
Grandfather—though at heart a warrior still—had been
forced to take his daughter and two remaining grandchil-
dren to the white soldiers so that Slender Woman could
have her baby in safety. Niño could not remember how
many days it had been since he had seen his father killed
by the white men. He yearned to tell Red Band how
grateful he was for his training, and now he never could.

But, he thought sleepily, the love that I feel for my
father is unchanged and I will yet prove myself worthy to
be his son.

# The River Crossing

THE NEXT morning Niño sat on the floor and ate his breakfast beans in a corner of the bustling ranch house kitchen. Then he, Don Armando, and Miguel set forth once more.

Their way took them farther south under a deep blue sky between snowcapped mountains and along paths bounded by good-sized junipers and dense thorny chaparral. The sun sparkled on clean white patches of snow and the air was as crisp and clear and heady as the water of a mountain spring. The horses pranced and sidestepped, resenting the curbing bits in their mouths and the governing reins on their necks.

Niño knew exactly how they felt. He, too, wanted to run free across this shining land, but he knew that this was not the time. Although Don Armando had not bound him in ropes, he watched him closely every minute. In any case, there was nowhere to go but along the path. So dense were the thickets on either side that the horse's flesh—and his own legs—would have been cut to ribbons if he tried to push through them.

40

Behind him Don Armando and Miguel talked with a good natured teasing and comradeship that made Niño's heart ache with memories. Though he and Red Band had not chattered so—such was not the way of the Navajo— they, too, had often ridden mile after mile, each knowing the heart of the other. And as Don Armando frequently instructed Miguel in some point, so had Red Band instructed his son.

But here the similarity between Red Band and Don Armando ended. Whereas Red Band had accepted and loved both of his sons equally, Don Armando quite obviously found little to admire in his other son, Tomás. The boy's name came up occasionally in the conversations, but always Miguel was heaped with praise, while Tomás was treated with scorn. Niño wondered about this other son. What could make him so ill-favored?

Miguel ignored Niño, never speaking, but as much as Niño despised the cool arrogance of this boy who strutted like a courting jaybird, he nevertheless remembered that in the eating place, while everyone else had laughed at his misery, Miguel had ordered water given to him.

"Have you worked with horses?" Don Armando asked him abruptly after they had ridden a long time.

Niño nodded.

"Then let Jake have him, Papá," Miguel suggested. "He'll be able to handle him." Don Armando mumbled something under his breath.

No more was said to Niño the rest of the day. He had much time to consider this Jake person for whom he would work. Visions of Manuel floated before his mind and he remembered the starvation and the agony of the rope. Indians could be cruel to their enemies, he knew. But they never directed their savagery at children. With Mexicans, however, he could expect neither kindness nor mercy, and the man in the eating place had said this Jake was surly, one not to be trusted.

He had to get away soon, before he reached the hacienda. Uncle had said it was almost impossible for a slave to get free once he became trapped behind those high adobe walls.

Rising at dawn and eating breakfast at the haciendas they stayed at each night, then setting forth with Niño a little in the lead, no one speaking to him mile after mile—this became the pattern as they rode steadily southward. The weather grew milder, and the mountains finally disappeared in a blue haze behind them. Niño's neck began to heal and the constant pain subsided.

At one point in the trail Niño spotted a cactus growing beside the trail. Many times, when Red Band had forced him to find his own food, he had peeled and eaten the flat fleshy cactus pads, both as food and for the liquid they contained. He was thirsty, so without dismounting from the little mare, he slid over to one side, hooked a leg around its neck, and grabbed a pad and snapped it off. Easily, in the way taught to him by Red Band, he slid back into position and peeled the thorny skin from the pad before he ate it.

Glancing back at his captors while the juice dribbled on his chin, he saw Miguel watching him with a trace of admiration that he quickly hid.

But he did not let himself forget for one minute what Uncle had told him—to the Spaniards, the Mexicans, and the white man, an Indian was less important than an animal and he was treated as such.

One morning they paused on the edge of a low mesa. In the distance they could see a meandering line of trees cutting across the high desert and Niño knew they were approaching water of some sort.

Don Armando lifted his field glasses and watched a cloud of dust in the distance. "We will wait here," he said.

"Is it danger, Papá?" Miguel asked.

"No, but we will rest awhile."

As the dust settled, Niño could see a large group of wagons and horsemen milling around on the bank of a wide river that glistened like silver in the sun. He could hear the faint sounds of men's cries urging people and animals into the water as they headed for the opposite bank. He watched two riders detach themselves from the others and gallop along the river a short distance, shouting and waving, and then return.

At last they were all across and Don Armando straightened in the saddle. "Let's go," he said. "And you, Niño—when we get to the Rio Grande, hang on to the mare. She'll get you across."

Niño nodded. Although he had played in the shallow waters of the river in Tsegi Canyon, he did not know how to swim and he was glad he didn't have to learn today in a river as big as this one!

There were five ragged Mexicans lounging under a great

bare cottonwood when Niño, Miguel, and Don Armando reached the river's edge.

"Who were all those people?" Miguel asked them.

One old man shrugged and continued to pick his teeth. "Oh them—just another bunch of stinking Navajos on their way to Bosque Redondo."

Niño's heart ached with sudden longing for his people— his home—his family.

"A girl and a woman were swept away," the old man went on. "The soldiers couldn't stop to help them and they were lost."

Don Armando shrugged. "No matter," he said indifferently and, pointing to the river, added, "We cross here."

Niño looked fearfully at the muddy water that moved rapidly. This same river had carried away two of his people. Would it dislodge him from this small horse?

Miguel and his roan went first, then Niño plunged his mare into the water. Strengthened by his hatred of men who could let such things happen to women and children just because they were Indians, he clung with all his might to his horse. He felt the icy water swirl around his waist, numbing him, and it pulled at his legs as it tried to lift him from the back of the mare.

Miguel was already on the bank pouring water out of his boot when Niño came out of the river well ahead of Don Armando. To his right was a shallow wash, and, driven by his hate for the Spaniard and his fierce desire for freedom, Niño dug his heels into the mare and headed for it. Winded though it was from the crossing, the little horse responded and raced over the sandy bottom of the wash.

Don Armando yelled, but Niño kept going, though he knew he was doing a foolhardy thing—Don Armando had that gun at his waist. But he would rather die a warrior than live as a slave to this despised man. The mare could outswim the gelding, so if he could get back to the river and cross it, he would have a chance.

He headed up the side of the wash. Once on open land he turned back to the Rio Grande. He was almost in the middle of the river before Don Armando appeared on the bank behind him. Niño looked hopefully at the opposite shore. It was a boulder-strewn and hilly place, so if he could reach those hills it would be possible for him to lose Don Armando.

There was a loud hissing sound and before he could identify it, his arms were bound to his sides and he was jerked from his horse. As the water closed over his head, he realized Don Armando hadn't even needed his gun. He had that rope!

Choking and sputtering, unable to breathe, Niño was dragged through the water and up onto the bank. In one fluid movement Don Armando dismounted, grabbed him, and ripped off the rope. He lifted him in the air and slammed him flat on the ground.

"You try that again and I'll kill you," he roared. "Understand?"

Niño ignored him, trying to breathe after having the wind knocked out of him.

Don Armando was livid with rage at his silence. "Did you really think you could get away from me that easily? This time I'm going to teach you a lesson."

He kicked Niño over with his boot. Then he raised his riding whip and brought the thick leather thongs down on Niño's back. Again and again he lashed at Niño until his deerskin shirt was shredded and his flesh was bloody and raw.

Niño tried to crawl away. He rolled onto his back to protect it from further damage. He dodged and flinched. He did everything but cry out. That he would never do.

"Scream, you stubborn Indian," Don Armando said through clenched teeth. "Scream!"

"Papá!" Miguel gasped. "No! Stop!"

Finally, when it seemed Niño could no longer keep his anguish from passing his lips, Don Armando hit him over the head with the whip handle and Niño plunged gratefully into unconsciousness.

He was shivering when he came to. His clothes were wet and he could not remember why as he struggled to his feet, holding onto the trunk of a cottonwood to steady his spinning world. He reached for his wet blanket and threw it over his shoulders and the pain made him wince as he remembered.

When he looked up, he saw Miguel astride the blue roan, his face pale, as though sick at the sight of the torn and bloody back. Don Armando was leading the mare along the river bank and stopped before him. "Get on the horse."

Choking on his hatred, Niño tried to mount. He fell back and smothered a moan as the blanket rubbed against his wounds.

"Get on the horse," Don Armando said again.

Making a tremendous effort, Niño mounted and looked across at the Spaniard. Their eyes met and locked and in that moment Niño knew that he had scored a personal victory. Don Armando had beaten him senseless, yet he had not been able to force a word or a cry from him.

He knew he could not continue his silence—he would have to talk eventually. But now the decision to speak would be his.

"So small a thing, my father," Niño thought in his bruised and aching heart. "But I shall do better."

That night his sleep was broken by feverish dreams, and the next day his pain was almost more than he could bear. Sometimes he was hardly aware he was on horseback. Behind him Don Armando and Miguel rode in unaccustomed silence, speaking only occasionally. Late in the afternoon, Niño watched white clouds drifting overhead and he remembered the Navajo legends he'd heard around the hogan fires during the long winter nights—stories about Father Sun who gave light, Changing Woman who governed the seasons, Turquoise Woman who gave them their sky blue stones for protection, Spider Woman who watched over them, and the Lightning god who gave speed to man. Every day his people sang chants and prayers to their gods, thanking them for the sun, the crops, their homes, their very existence. They tried to live at peace with nature. If they failed—if this peaceful co-existence became upset—they asked the *hatali*, the Medicine Man, to sing a ceremonial chant that would drive out the evil spirits and bring them back into harmony with nature.

"But I have no *hatali*," thought Niño. "And I do not know what to do." He felt very small and lonely.

Then, unbidden, a chant came to his mind and he began to sing softly, calling his gods to drive out the evil spirits that were torturing his body, and to protect him in this new and alien land. A lovely peace moved over him as he sang and he felt enveloped in a tender warmth.

"Stop that horrible, heathen noise," Don Armando said crossly.

Niño stopped. It did not matter—in his heart he was at home.

# *Jake*

FROM the note of anticipation in Miguel's voice, Niño knew when they started out in the morning that this was the last day of their journey. It had been many days since he had last seen his beloved canyon, though the traveling had been leisurely as they rode in a zig-zag course from one hacienda to another, and he wondered how far he was from his home. Although his back was only a little better, he no longer felt as if he were going to fall from his horse at any minute.

So much of the conversation behind him had to do with horses, and Niño wondered where Don Armando kept the big herds he spoke of. Certainly Niño had not seen any grazing in the desert land they were riding across, although he had noticed droppings along the trail, so many that it seemed as if a herd had been driven there. The droppings were hard and dry, put there many many days before.

"The hacienda and its fields must be bigger than anything I can imagine," he thought, "if that many horses graze inside the walls."

49

Uncle had told him that the adobe walls always encircled not only the buildings but the fields and the pastures as well. Some haciendas were not very large, such as a few that Niño had seen on their travels southward—a house or two, a garden, and maybe a few acres of pasture.

But Niño remembered Tale Teller's description of the elaborate haciendas of the very wealthy landowners. "There was always one large house—a grand one for the *patrón*—and many smaller houses for the slaves, the horses, the *peóns*, sometimes a separate small one for the overseer, and special ones for the guests of the *patrón*. Beyond these buildings were the fields and orchards often stretching as far as a man could see. And around it all there was always that great adobe wall. "This was to keep raiding Indians out," Uncle had said grimly, then added his own bitter conclusion, "and to keep the slave Indians in."

When the sun was straight overhead, they topped a slight rise and there, spread in the flat valley below them, was the hacienda. With sinking heart Niño studied the wall that seemed to encompass most of the valley. A man standing on a tall horse would not be able to see over it! Outside the wall the open land was sparsely covered with mesquite, sage and bunch grass, good for grazing cattle and horses.

Inside the wall near the western end was the big house, a glistening white building of many arches that formed a huge square around a tree-studded yard. The house was larger and more elaborate than anything Niño had ever seen, and he wondered with amazement how people could find comfort and ease in anything so big. With deep longing he thought of his small round hogan that had seemed to fold protectively around its little family.

Behind the house many adobe buildings of various sizes were scattered about, and he noticed one with a wooden cross on the top. In the grassless, open area between the buildings he could see many people. Eastward from the buildings the plowed fields spread away in orderly rows and on the west small trees marched stiffly all the way to the wall. Beyond the fields and orchards lay uncultivated land that looked like good pasture. At one end of the grazing land, hidden from the house area by a thick row of trees, was a pond that shimmered silvery in the bright sunlight. But once again Niño was puzzled. He saw only a scattering of animals grazing within the walled area. Where were the vast herds Don Armando had talked about?

The front entrance to the hacienda faced west and it was toward this that they headed when Don Armando touched the mare's flank with his riding crop. "Move along," he said impatiently. "Quickly, now!"

As they loped toward the huge wrought-iron gate, it swung open and a dainty little girl ran toward them. She was about eleven, too, Niño thought, but much smaller than he. On a chain around her neck hung a big silver cross with a turquoise stone set in it.

"Papá! Miguel! Welcome home!"

Don Armando leaned down and scooped her up onto his horse, holding her close, and Miguel reached over to touch her long dark hair, murmuring, "It is good to be home, Lucia *mía*."

A young boy—older than the girl and maybe even slightly older than Miguel—stood in the gateway watching them.

"Welcome home, Papá and Miguel," he said in a low voice as his father rode past him without a word. Miguel nodded, calling out, *"Hola,* Tomás."

Niño glanced back. So this was Tomás! No wonder Don Armando preferred his other son. This one was skinny with very pale skin and he seemed almost to shrink when spoken to. His large dark eyes stared out at a world he evidently disliked.

A doll-like, exquisite woman came behind Tomás and put her arm around his shoulder, gently pulling him toward the others. She wore a long gray skirt and a bright yellow blouse. In her black hair was a tall comb which supported a black cloth as delicate as a spider's web that fell in folds to her shoulders.

"Welcome home, my husband, and dear Miguel," she said warmly. Then she looked toward her son. "Tomás has been waiting here all morning, watching for your return."

Don Armando's eyes narrowed. "Indeed," he said, letting the little girl slide to the ground and dismounting beside the woman. "And would not a proper son mount a horse and ride out to meet his father?"

"I would not let him go because of the Indians."

"That is why I keep insisting that he must learn to use a gun." His eyes searched her face. "How are you, Teresa, my love?" Obviously satisfied with what he saw, he smiled and turned to his son. "Tomás," he acknowledged his presence. Nothing more.

Several Mexicans, dressed in white pants and shirts with bright red sashes around their waists, gathered the weary horses. No one paid any attention to Niño as he sat aching on his horse while the big gates were locked behind him. He watched in wonder at the gentleness of this Spaniard with the women in his family and at his pride in them. But not in this other son—and that was strange.

"Hello, Jake," Miguel spoke with such genuine friendliness that Niño turned, curious about the hated Mexican he would work for. But he was even more interested in what kind of person could evoke such good will out of the cold Spanish boy.

Standing by one of the arches was a rangy man wearing a soiled gray hat pushed so far back on his head that it seemed to be hanging from the thick wiry hair. A sweat-stained vest hung carelessly over a red-checkered wool shirt. Although his skin was tanned until it was the red-brown of a polished piñon nut, the squinting blue eyes and the corn tassel hair, as well as the line of pale skin on his forehead where his hat usually fitted, proclaimed this man as white!

Instinctively Niño stiffened, remembering his father's death.

"Hi, Mike," Jake said cheerfully in Spanish. "Sure good to see you back. Missed you."

"His name is Miguel," Don Armando said stiffly. "How many times must I tell you that?"

Niño sensed antagonism between these two men and

remembered José's comment about the overseer's hate for Don Armando. Vaguely he wondered why a Spaniard would hire a white man he hated to be his overseer. But then, Spaniards, Mexicans, and the white men always did things that made no sense.

Jake's face brightened as he turned back to Miguel. "How was the trip?"

"Great!" Miguel answered, his voice lively. "The most exciting thing happened, Jake. You should've seen it. You know how good a swimmer that mare is—well, going up she got away from me when we crossed the river." His dark eyes glowed as he stood close to Jake, his hands gesturing as he talked. "She took off—even loaded with all those skins. I had Papá's rope, so I went after her and roped her, Jake. Really I did."

"What kind of loop?" Jake asked, grinning.

"A California twist—like you taught me." Miguel laughed aloud. "Jake, it was exciting—just like a *vaquero*—"

"Miguel!" Don Armando's stern voice cut into his excited chatter. "Come."

"I'm proud of you, Mike," Jake said, sliding an arm across the boy's shoulder briefly. Then he turned away, made some teasing remark to Tomás, and before Niño was aware of it, he strode over and took hold of the mare's mane. Niño guessed he was older than Red Band, but not as old as Grandfather.

"What shall I do with this young'un?" Jake asked Don Armando.

"He's to work in the stables," Don Armando said indifferently. "See to it." He moved off with his family, the little girl dancing in front of him and the two boys following behind.

"Come on, young'un, let's get you settled in," Jake said and his hand moved from the horse's mane to its halter. Then he added, "But you probably don't understand Spanish, do you?"

"I understand," Niño said stiffly.

"Well, what do you know!" Jake lifted his hat and scratched his head. "Think you're the first young Indian I've ever known that did." He led the horse past the beautiful white arches through which Niño saw a long porch paved with colored tiles, and past clusters of brilliant flowers and lacy fern-like shrubs in big colored pots that contrasted sharply with the dazzling whitewash of the house. Despite his misery at being locked within these imprisoning walls, his Navajo love of the earth and all growing things made him react to the wild array of flowers.

How beautiful this earth is, he thought. So different from my canyon, but beautiful nevertheless.

Then they rounded the corner and the loveliness disappeared. Here there were no flowers and the buildings—although sturdy and well made—were mud colored. They went past these toward some shabby adobe buildings farther on. Many people milled around—Mexican women in black *rebozos*—shawls—hurrying here and there, their half-naked children stirring up dust as they romped, some men on horses, and others at work. He saw a few Indians repairing the supports of a strange thing with wooden blades that turned in the wind. They were men with the look of a wounded coyote with its tail between its legs. "Never will I be like that," he thought, defiant as always. Some of the people glanced his way, but there was little interest in one battered and mud-caked Indian boy.

Jake halted by a small shack and when Niño slid to the ground, Jake pushed him toward a doorway. Involuntarily Niño cried out.

"You hurt?" Jake asked anxiously. "Come on inside and let's see."

Inside the room, Niño let his blanket slip to the floor exposing his shredded shirt and torn back. Jake let out a long low whistle. "What've you been doing—fighting the *patrón*?"

"I would not talk."

One sunbleached eyebrow went up. "And for that he beat you?" He did not wait for a reply but pointed to a bench. "Lay on that—face down. I'll be right back." He went out of the room.

Niño darted to the doorway—escape his only thought, then he paused. Spreading beyond the shack were stables, cornfields, and finally the almost-empty pasture. Several women with black shawls stood talking by a well, and a stooped man in a long brown robe walked toward the building with a cross. Surrounding it all was that high wall. The red sandstone walls of his canyon were many, many times higher—so high that eagles soared below its rims—yet there he had never felt trapped. But here inside this adobe wall, his world suddenly closed in on him, making it hard for him to breathe. He knew there was no way of getting outside them.

"Oh, Changing Woman, mother of the earth, help me get out!" he gasped and felt his prayer unheard. In this alien place he could not feel close to the earth, and his gods seemed so far, far away. And he had no turquoise, no sacred pollen, no eagles' feathers—nothing. Wretched with despair and feeling deserted by everything familiar, he staggered back to the bench.

In a moment Jake returned, carrying a pan of steaming water. "Got it from the cook," he explained while he rummaged in a box until he found a jar of salve. He took a small knife from one of the many pockets in his vest and cut a rag from a larger piece of cloth. Then he began to soak the deerskin shirt until he could peel it away from Niño's skin.

Niño bit down savagely on his arm to keep from screaming. The cleaning was even more agonizing than the cutting of the whip that had caused the raw stripes. It took a long time, but finally the job was done. Jake cleaned the crusted sores on his neck, then spread the salve carefully on the open wounds—not as gently as Slender Woman would have done, but not roughly either, Niño grudgingly admitted.

When Jake was finished, he reached for a blue shirt that was hanging on a nearby peg. "Here, put this on." He wrinkled his nose as he looked at the torn blood-and-mud-stained deerskin shirt on the floor. "That one's about done for."

Niño sat up but he did not take the shirt. He did not want anything that belonged to a white man—even this one.

"Put it on," Jake insisted. "It'll keep the flies from crawling all over your open sores. You can't be hugging a blanket around you while you work." He looked thoughtfully at Niño, then tried again. "Look, it's not mine. Belonged to another Indian. He's dead—"

Terrified, Niño looked around the room. A man had died in here—the place was *chindi*! "In here?" he gasped. "Someone died in here?"

"No—no. Out beyond the wall. He tried to escape and Don Armando shot him."

Reluctantly Niño put on the shirt. It was very wrong to use anything belonging to someone who died—especially something so personal as his clothing. But he didn't know what else to do. He shivered, knowing full well that with each new thing he was forced to do, the evil spirits were closing in on him. How could he possibly last in this land of the Mexican and the white man? With painful longing he yearned to be back in the familiar and sacred canyon. It had not been too many days since he and New Found Boy had played with abandon, chasing the dog and climbing the rocks. Yet that life seemed almost like a dream now. His jaw muscles tightened and he stared down at his deerskin moccasins. "I will not let it become only a dream to me," he thought desperately. "I will remember everything. I will never forget I am Straight Arrow, the son of Red Band."

"What's your name?" Jake asked.

With a look of scorn that anyone could show so little courtesy as to ask a personal question like that, Niño stared at the white man. "Niño," he said defiantly.

Jake's eyebrow shot up again, then he shrugged. "Well, Niño, you'll be my, waddy—my helper. I'm the head honcho and I keep an eye on all of Don Armando's horses, his private ones as well as those he sells." He put one booted foot on the bench and rested an elbow on his knee. His bright blue eyes studied Niño closely and his face was stern. "There are a few things you'd better know. You'll take orders from me—take them and obey them. You'll bunk in the slaves' quarters, get your grub in the kitchen, and you will never go out into the front area—never—understand?"

"I understand," Niño said automatically, trying to figure out what sort of Spanish this white man spoke. Certainly he used many words Niño had never heard.

"Well, you mind it then. Don Armando won't have any Indians near his family, and no redskin has ever set foot inside the white house. The flogging you'll get for breaking that rule will make this one look like a gentle pat on the back." Jake paused. "Let's see—oh, yes, on Sundays the *padre* will try to make a Christian out of you until noon, then you'll work till evening." He dropped his foot to the ground and straightened. "Meantime, go see cook and get some grub. You look like a starving stray dog somebody found."

Niño hesitated, staring out the doorway at the distant hills. "Am I in Mexico?" he asked finally.

Jake shook his head. "Mexico is many days ride south of here. You're in my country—the United States. This part is called New Mexico Territory."

Niño's passive face showed none of his inner hope. The

name of Jake's country meant nothing to him, but if Mexico was still much farther south, then he was not as far from his canyon as he had thought.

As if Jake had read Niño's thoughts, he grunted. "You won't get beyond those walls, young'un, so forget it. The only place you're going right now is to the cook shack. Then come back here and I'll put you to work."

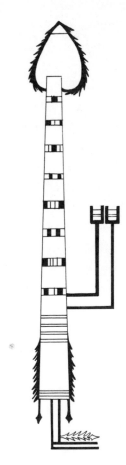

# The Pond

NIÑO resisted working for Jake, but the overseer's big brown hand, cuffing his head, soon changed his mind. Finally he had to admit that although Jake was far from gentle, he was not cruel. So, outwardly submissive, Niño did as he was told, but always uppermost in his thoughts was escape. As Red Band had said, to live in captivity was not the way of the Navajo, especially when the captor was a pretentious and arrogant Spaniard.

It was not until his back had healed that Niño realized Jake had been giving him only easy jobs to do. Finally Jake said that the cuts were scabbed over and there was no more need for the salve treatment. He put the jar in the box for the last time and turned to Niño.

"Take off your britches," he ordered.

Niño glowered, but he knew better than to risk a cuffing for refusing to obey, so he removed his deerskins. Jake tossed them in a corner and handed him a faded pair of tan cotton pants.

"You'll wear these from now on," he said.

"I want my deerskins."

Jake shook his head. "No. Don Armando's orders—no redskin trappings around here. Put on the pants."

Naked and shivering in the cold room, Niño said defiantly, "Navajos don't wear Mexican—Mexican trappings."

Jake suppressed a smile. "Can't you forget you're an Indian for once?"

"No!" Niño shouted. He snatched the pants and shoved one leg in angrily. He jammed his other leg in and hiked up the too-big pants, tying them at the waist with a rope Jake threw to him. "Could you forget you're a white man and think of yourself as a Navajo?"

Jake grinned widely, his even white teeth shining in his brown face. "Always waving the tomahawk, aren't you? Look, Niño, you're going to be here the rest of your life, so why don't you stop arching your back? The sooner you do, the easier it'll be on you. And everyone else!"

Niño pulled on the faded blue shirt and strode out without another word, stepping over a small dusty child who was playing in the doorway. "I am not going to be here the rest of my life," he told himself. "And I am not going to forget I am a Navajo—a warrior!"

He knew what happened to those who did forget. Like Felipe and Esteban, the two Utes who shared his small room. They had become pale shadows of their Mexican masters, walking with bowed heads, speaking broken Spanish instead of their own language, and praying to a little statue they called the Virgin Mary. In their desire to please, they had even cut their hair, and they constantly prodded Niño to do the same. But Niño stubbornly refused to do away with his heavy *chonga* knot or remove the yellow headband. Nor would he wear the thick shoes the Utes clumped around in. A Navajo wore moccasins. Besides, these had been made by Red Band, and it was all he had left of his father.

He passed the well on his way to the stables, yearning for a drink of the cold, sweet water. But several Mexican women were there and he had already learned that even these lowly *peóns* would not allow the Indian slaves to come near them. If he should dare, the fat one with wide flaring nostrils would swing her pail at his head as she had done before.

With a sigh he dodged among the chickens scratching in the dirt and went to feed the horses. There his misery subsided the way it always did when he was with the animals. He sometimes thought the love he felt for them was the only good thing left in his life.

The next day just before dawn, Jake awakened him. "Come on—get up, Niño," he said. "Today you learn to work like a man."

Esteban and Felipe sat up on their sheepskins and grinned—and he knew what their grins meant—now this proud Navajo would find out what it really meant to be a slave.

He followed Jake out into the half-dark world. Somewhere a rooster crowed and a dog barked. The air smelled of sage and woodsmoke, which meant the cook was in her kitchen. Arrows of pale light pierced the blackness and Niño knew that soon the land would be bathed in golden sunshine. Every morning of his life he had gone outside the hogan just as the world awoke, to listen to his father or grandfather sing the chant of welcome to Father Sun. He longed to do it here, but it was forbidden. The stooped old man in the long brown robe—the *padre*—had said it was barbaric and the work of the devil, and any Indian heard chanting would be flogged.

They went first to the well to draw water, which Niño carried in buckets to the saddle horses in the nearer stables. He lost count of how many times he had to go back and forth. After he had filled the feed bins so the horses could eat, he had his own breakfast of beans and tortillas.

"First the animals," he thought, "and then the Indian." But he did not really care because he loved the horses.

He cleaned the stalls and polished the tack until it shone. When everything was spotless he drew more water, and this time carried it to the stables out by the cornfields. Here were kept the horses used by the *vaqueros* and other workers. These stables were twice as far from the well as the first ones and there were many more horses so that he would have been glad of a rest when he finished hauling the water.

One thing continued to puzzle him—he had still not seen any large herds. When he had questioned Jake, he was told gruffly that Don Armando had recently sold a big herd of horses and had not yet replenished his stock. Niño was sure there was something odd about the whole thing—Jake had acted so strangely.

But he had little time to think about it. Besides doing

the feeding and cleaning and polishing, there was water to be hauled for the house and for the cook, a brief midday meal exactly like breakfast, then hoeing in the cornfields all afternoon with the other Indians. When he finally crawled into his sheepskin, he had no more energy to think or plan or even to dream. He could only pull his blanket close about him before he fell into the deep sleep of utter exhaustion.

He came at last to a time when he was no longer so tired at the end of the day that he fell immediately to sleep. Then sometimes he would lie restless on his sheepskin listening to the night sounds—the cry of a hunting owl, the song of a prowling coyote, the chirping of a happy cricket.

One night there was a sound different from all others—and it came from the big house. Niño thought that it must be the music they all talked about—Tomás' music. It did not sound like any music he had ever heard, yet it touched him deeply, and something about it made the ache in his heart more painful than ever. He crept to the doorway of his room so that he could hear it more clearly, and just then he saw Don Armando gallop past him to the stables. Someone was squatting beside the wall and got up to grab the reins as Don Armando jumped from his horse.

"We did not expect you back until tomorrow." It was Jake's voice.

"Obviously not—since I hear Tomás at that blasted guitar."

"It does no harm, Armando," Jake said soothingly. "I think it's even good for the boy. . . ."

"How could you know what is good for my son,
you—you Yanqui *vaquero*! And don't call me Armando—you
forget your place."

There was no warmth in the sound of Jake's laughter.
"Yes, sir, Don Armando, sir." It was a mockery of respect
and it made Niño wonder what there was between these
two men that held them together when there was so much
hate.

The music in the house stopped abruptly when Don
Armando entered.

As the weeks passed, Niño saw Don Armando many
times riding about the hacienda, but always the many
Indians seemed to melt into the ground when he rode
past. They knew the fury of his long whip if they dared
allow themselves to remain openly in his sight, especially
if Miguel, Tomás, or occasionally Lucia, rode with the
*patrón*.

The cold of winter vanished and Niño wistfully watched
the big cottonwoods don their new leaves. The peach trees
in the orchard and the one near the kitchen fluffed their
pink blossoms in the breeze, and in the cornfields where
he worked endlessly with other slaves like himself, little
green fingers burst out of the rich soil and pointed to the
sun. Birds were building their nests, adding their musical
chatter to the everyday sounds of the squeaking windmill,
or the creak of wagon wheels, or the easy singing of the
Mexicans. And the air was filled with the scent of lemon
blossoms.

Most of these signs of spring were achingly familiar to

Niño, a time when Changing Woman, grown old with winter, suddenly became young again. He yearned to chant loudly to her, to give his thanks for her generous gifts.

More and more Jake gave him work that involved the horses. "You have a gentle hand with animals," he explained and began teaching Niño how to doctor wounds, treat colic, and even how to shoe the horses. It was work Niño loved, and he listened attentively to Jake's instructions.

One dawn in early summer, he entered the distant stables just as the scrawny mare he'd ridden from Santa Fe was about to throw a foal. Niño knelt beside her, crooning softly in Navajo until the filly was born. She was an ugly mud-yellow in color and even more spindly than most newborn foals.

"She will not be a favorite here," he said to Jake who had come right after the birth and now helped the wobbly-legged filly get to her feet. "Only pretty horses are favored by the *patrón's* family—the lively kind."

Jake glanced at Niño's bitter face. "Shucks, everybody's worth something," he said, giving a lopsided grin. "Take that mare, for instance. Now she's about as puny a critter as you'll ever see. But she can outswim any big stallion in this hacienda. That's why she goes north with Don Armando to Santa Fe."

He continued to help the filly, even as the mare eyed him belligerently. "Horses—people—all alike," he said with a shrug. "Take Tomás. Like this filly—quiet, not much to look at. Won't even try to ride properly—mostly to gall his pa. But when it comes to music. . . ." Jake whistled softly. "Now there's where he shines—a real artist, that one."

He backed away from the filly as it stumbled over to the mare. "Mike—now he's a different horse altogether— more like the *patrón's* gelding—haughty as a skunk with its flag up. Only difference is, Mike's got a soft heart—hates cruelty. And he likes horses, not just to buy and sell, but to ride and handle. Yes sir, he's a first-rate horseman."

He filled the bin with grain. "And you—you're sorta like this mare—scrawny, but with more determination and guts than a cougar on the prowl." He looked directly at Niño, his blue eyes steady. "I've broke the meanest horses in my time. And I found that there's always some good in them. I kinda use that idea on folks, too. Even Don Armando's not all bad."

"How?" asked Niño in disbelief.

But Jake had already turned away as several Mexican children came running in to see him and to admire the new filly.

Niño watched Jake with the children. Even these little Mexicans—children of the *peóns*—were special in his sight, each one worthy in some way. Niño looked back at the mare. It truly was useless looking—but he remembered the way it outswam the big gelding and the way it responded to his drumming heels, tired as it had been. And Jake said he was like the mare.

His head rose slightly and the unworthiness that months of slavery had piled on him fell away. Until now he hadn't realized how he had let the continual indifference, the floggings, and the contempt beat him down, until like the others, he considered himself unworthy—merely Niño, the Indian slave. Again he remembered—he was Straight Arrow, the son of a great warrior. He must never let himself forget that. And he was forced to admit that, although Jake was a white man, he was good.

Following Jake's comments, Niño began making things harder and harder for himself. He never walked when he could run, never sat when he could stand, never carried less when he could handle more. At first his arms and back and legs complained painfully, but soon they began to accept the burdens he imposed on them. His muscles developed great strength and his lungs responded to whatever demands he made. He knew his father would be pleased.

On rare occasions Niño noticed Jake strolling near the white house, chatting pleasantly with Miguel or Tomás, although Don Armando never seemed pleased when he found them together.

One hot day when Niño was working in the farthest cornfield with a group of slaves, his brown muscular back glistening with sweat, he heard the faint sound of laughter over by the distant pond. He recognized the voices of Tomás and Miguel. Because the two Spanish boys rarely ever came over to this part of the hacienda, and because it was the first time he'd ever heard them really laughing happily, he was curious as to what was going on. Glancing around, he didn't see either Jake or Francisco. When the Indians near him were looking elsewhere, he darted into the brush and silently moved among the palo verde and the low-growing bushes. He grinned when he realized he

was automatically moving with the stealth taught to him
by Red Band. And for a moment he forgot his months of
slavery as he imagined himself sneaking up on a Ute
Indian to steal his horse. But the vision vanished when he
heard the familiar deeper rumble of Jake's voice.
Nevertheless he continued his caution, hiding any trail so
he could not be pursued. In this huge expanse of walled
land, he could remain hidden for a long time if he needed
to.

He moved some low branches of a big creosote bush
carefully and lowered himself to the ground, letting them
fold back over him. By lying on his stomach he could peer
out from under the branches and see the pond. The still
water reflected the cloudless blue sky, and all around the
edges the reflections made a double picture of shrubs and
trees growing up and down.

"All right, boys, into the water," Jake ordered.

In the shade of a big mesquite Niño saw Miguel and
Tomás taking off their clothes. Beside them was Jake, his
naked body starkly white, his face, neck, and hands a
deep brown.

The two boys ran to the edge of the water and stopped.
Gingerly Miguel began to inch his way in. "It's still too
cold," he said, shivering.

Jake chuckled and gave him a shove, and Miguel
tumbled into the water gasping and thrashing about.

"In with you," he threatened Tomás and the pale-
skinned boy dodged the out-thrust arm to plunge into the
pond.

For a long time Niño lay unmoving, watching them

enviously, while Jake tried to show them how to do
something he called a dog paddle. Homesickness saddened
him as he remembered how he and New Found Boy had
often cooled themselves by splashing in the creek.

"Mike, kick your feet," Jake yelled in exasperation.
"Kick—look, see how Tomás is doing it?"

Miguel glanced at the other boy and his face clouded.
"Maybe he can swim, but he sure can't ride like a. . . ."

"Yes, Mike, we all know you're a good *caballero*," Jake
said evenly, "but Tomás, he's a good. . . ."

"He's good for nothing," Miguel snapped peevishly,
throwing himself back on the water and kicking water
toward Jake.

". . . a good musician," Jake went on calmly.

Miguel stood up. "That is nothing to my father."

"He is *not* your father," Tomás snorted. "He is mine!
*Your* father was Don Ernesto. And you're not even my
brother—only my cousin." He dove under the water.

Niño was amazed. Miguel was not truly the son of Don
Armando! Yet they were so alike—he did not understand
it. And how could Don Armando love Miguel, who was
not his son, more than he loved Tomás, who was? He
tried to imagine Red Band doing such a thing and he
couldn't.

It was true that Tomás was quiet and usually un-
pleasant —not at all like the handsome and lively Miguel.
But he did make beautiful music.

Jake's cheerful voice cut across his thoughts. "Brother—
cousin—same difference as long as you're friends. That's
the important thing." Jake cupped his big hands and sent

showers of shimmering water over them both. "Come on,"
he shouted, "let's race!"

Laughing and kicking—the quarrel forgotten—they
churned the water to a white froth.

Tomás was the first to tire. He lay on his back in the
water with his hands folded under his head and floated
peacefully. "Why can't we just float around like this all the
time, Jake? Why do we have to learn to swim?"

"Every time Don Armando goes up to Santa Fe and
takes you young'uns with him, you have to cross the Rio
Grande." Jake flipped his head so that his thick wet hair
sent out a sparkling spray of water. "It's plain good horse
sense to know how to swim." Then he added almost under
his breath, "Besides, I worry about you both."

The boys looked at each other and smiled. And in that
moment Niño thought they looked like brothers, friendly
brothers who were not pitted against each other at all
because they were equally loved.

The jingling of spurs drove out all thoughts of the
Spanish boys. Niño knew that sound—Francisco! The
swarthy Mexican with the drooping mustache and cruel
dark eyes seemed to delight in proving to Jake that Niño
was totally incompetent and worthy only of flogging. From
the Utes in his room, Niño had learned that when
Francisco was only a boy, his father had been scalped by
the Mescalero Apaches, and from that time on Francisco
despised all Indians and never overlooked a chance to flog
one. The deep scars on Esteban's back were proof of
Francisco's intense hate.

Moving silently and ever so slowly, Niño drew his

moccasined feet in under the bush and waited, not breathing. Just a short distance away Francisco burst noisily out of the brush. Niño could not see him but he knew from the gloating sound of his voice that Francisco's eyes glittered with satisfaction at what he saw.

"Aha!" he exclaimed. "I'll wager the *patrón* knows nothing of such behavior!"

Jake and the boys spun around guiltily and one by one they stood up in the shallow area, their bodies dripping in silvery streams of water.

"Wait till the *patrón* hears of this," Francisco continued. "I think he has had just about enough of your insolence, Jake."

While Francisco spoke, Jake sloshed out of the pond and struggled into his pants. Francisco strode past Niño's tiny viewpoint and halted before the overseer. "You are not supposed. . . ."

To Niño's surprise, Jake grabbed the front of the big Mexican's shirt threateningly. Francisco was a half a head taller and much heavier, but at that moment the cold fury in Jake's eyes made him seem huge. It was the first time Niño had seen Jake really angry. "I would not be the one to tell him, if I were you."

Francisco shook off his hand. "He should get rid of you," he growled.

"But he won't," Jake said with a harsh laugh. He turned to the boys still in the water. "Get dressed, young'uns, lessons are over for today." He spun back to Francisco, "Git—and don't come sneaking around here anymore, you. . . ."

Francisco backed away, and his face took on a look of innocence. "I was not sneaking. I was looking for the Indian—Niño. He is gone."

"Gone?" Jake was puzzled. "Gone where?"

Francisco shrugged. "How should I know? He is not where he ought to be—in the field with the others."

"Then go look in the stables. Maybe a horse needed care."

Francisco looked defiantly at Jake. "He has escaped, I tell you. *Now* the *patrón* will. . ."

"Escaped?" Jake laughed. "How? All the gates are closed and he is much too small to go over that wall. Get on with you—go on—git!"

Grumbling, Francisco moved away, almost stepping on Niño, he passed by so closely. Jake continued to talk to the boys as if nothing had happened and Niño inched his way out from the bushes, covering any sign that he had been there. Quickly and silently he headed back to the fields, skirting the area where Jake and the boys would go to get their tethered horses.

When Jake rode out to the cornfields a short while later with an angry Francisco right behind him, Niño was busy at work, his brown back bent as he hoed the rich soil.

"Where have you been?" Jake demanded as soon as he rode up.

"Been?" Niño looked up innocently. "Why, here."

Jake turned accusing eyes at Francisco. "You weren't searching, you were sneaking. Now get over to the windmill and put some grease on it like I told you to. It's squealing like a pig in a bog."

With a look of hate at Niño, Francisco wheeled his
horse and rode off. Before Jake followed him he glanced
quzzically at Niño, who immediately went back to hoeing.
Niño watched him ride away, half smiling and half
puzzled. It was very strange, this Jake and the *patrón*.
Don Armando hated his overseer, yet he would not get
rid of him.

Then a new thought came to Niño. Maybe *would* was
not the right word. Maybe it was *dared* not. Niño
smiled—the thought was intriguing.

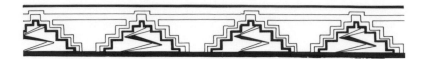

# The Blue Turquoise

ONE SUMMER morning, just as Niño finished cleaning the stables near the big house, there was a clink of spurs and Don Armando strode into the yard, followed by his children.

"Hit the trail, Niño—and you, too, Juan," Jake said quietly.

Silently Niño moved away. Then curiosity overcame his fear of being cuffed for disobedience and he hid behind a wagon to watch, while Juan, a cowed Apache slave with a whip-scarred back, disappeared beyond the stables.

Lucia entered behind her father, wearing a dove-gray riding dress and a black broadbrimmed hat. Around her neck hung the same silver cross with its turquoise stone that Niño had noticed the first time he saw her. It was beautiful, but not as beautiful, he thought, as his own handcrafted silver belt.

Niño sighed. So much evil had befallen them all since they stripped themselves of their sky blue stones. This stone Lucia wore was the only bit of turquoise he'd seen since he left Tsegi Canyon.

Behind Lucia came Miguel, resplendent in a suit the

76

color of a robin's egg and trimmed as always with the silver thread. Beside him Tomás looked like a tired and dusty crow. They were quiet until their horses were ready, then they started for the front gateway. Francisco, his arm cradling a rifle, went along to help discourage any marauding Indians that might appear.

Watching them, Niño began to laugh. That Tomás rode as though he had never been on a horse before—bouncing around like a leaf going downstream, pulled this way and that by the current. By contrast, Miguel rode like a *caballero*, sure of himself and his frisky horse.

When they were out of sight, Niño ran to the well for his buckets of water. He thought that he would rather be what he was—Straight Arrow, the captive Navajo, proud son of Red Band—than Tomás, miserable free son of Don Armando. Besides, some day *he* would be the free son of Red Band, and poor Tomás would never be anything more than he was today.

Jake, Niño and Juan worked together in the *vaqueros'* stables until the family returned from their ride and Jake had to go to the front stable to help them dismount. When he came back, he sent Niño to unsaddle the sweaty horses and brush them down while he finished wrapping the cut leg of one of the work horses. Francisco was busy currying his own mount, so when Niño reached the front stables, he found himself entirely alone. He murmured to the animals, loving the familiar smell of the stables. Only here was he happy.

While he brushed Don Armando's beautiful big bay, he hummed one of his Navajo chants. Then he turned to

Lucia's piebald and his eye was attracted by a gleam of light in the straw. Bending down to examine it more closely, he saw that it was the silver cross.

Furtively he glanced around, but there was no one in sight. He picked it up and darted inside the dark stall. With a quick twist of his strong hands he bent the cross so that the stone was loosened and fell into one palm. Elated to be once more holding a piece of the precious turquoise in his hand, he threw the cross to the ground. But he picked it up again almost immediately. He had to get rid of it. But where?

His searching eyes fell on a narrow space between the panels of two stalls that stood back to back. He dropped the cross into the opening then scooped up two handsful of dirt and threw them on top of it. It could only be found, he thought with satisfaction, if someone tore down the wall.

Jake's voice came to him from just beyond the stables. He had to decide what to do with the stone—quickly! They would all be back, he was sure, when Lucia discovered her loss, and they'd be certain he had stolen her beautiful cross. They'd search him. . . .

Frantically he tried to think of a safe place to hide his turquoise. He knew he was taking a great risk—it might even cost him his life if he were caught. Slaves had been shot for a lot less. But he had to have this stone because he needed it to help him get back home.

Jake's footsteps came closer and suddenly Niño decided what to do. He pulled off his dirty yellow headband and loosened the knot. Tucking the precious turquoise inside, he tightened it once more and slipped the band over his black hair.

When Jake came in, he was currying the piebald. Joy filled his rapidly beating heart, and for the first time in weeks, he truly felt like a warrior again. The turquoise would drive out the evil spirits that had plagued him for so long.

"Niño," Jake said, "high-tail it out to the cornfields."

Niño started out, his step lighter and his head higher than it had been in many months.

"Wait a minute," Jake called. "Come back here."

Niño went and stood in front of him, but Jake's questioning eyes stared at him so long that Niño finally looked down.

"What've you been up to? You have a maverick look. You're not planning some darned fool thing, are you—like maybe trying to escape?"

Niño shook his head.

Jake continued to stare at him, and Niño forced himself to meet the puzzled gaze with his usual defiant look.

"Oh, go on—get to work," Jake growled finally.

He had been working in the cornfield only a short time when Francisco appeared. "Jake wants you back at the stable. *Pronto*! Don Armando is there, too, and he's powerful mad. What kind of trouble you been into now?" he asked with relish.

Niño didn't bother to reply, but he was conscious of the others around him eyeing him with malicious interest. He reached the stables, breathing hard, and as he saw Don Armando's scowling face, he felt himself shrink in a moment of terror. Lucia was staring at him accusingly. Tomás leaned against one of the stalls, teasing a big white stable cat. His glance at Niño was one of frank curiosity. Miguel stood apart, looking worried. Niño felt his insides tremble as he faced these Spaniards.

"What did you do with my daughter's silver cross?" Don Armando demanded.

"Cross? I know nothing of any cross."

"You're lying. Search him, Jake."

Jake ran his hands over Niño's body, feeling around his neck, in his waistband, and his pockets. "He doesn't have it."

"But he must have it," Lucia insisted. "Look in his moccasins."

Niño removed his moccasins and handed them to Jake. Jake shook his head.

"Untie that filthy knot of hair," Don Armando was obviously annoyed that the search was proving futile.

With fingers that were close to trembling, Niño unwound the string around the chonga knot at the nape of his neck. His long black hair fell untidily on his shoulders.

"He wouldn't dare take the cross," Jake said to Don Armando. "He knows he'd be in as much trouble as though he grabbed the hot end of a branding iron if he did."

"Any time a thieving Indian would let that stop him—take off that headband."

"He couldn't hide anything as big as that. . ." Jake began.

"Take it off!"

Jake grabbed the band by the knot and yanked it off, shaking it as he did so. Niño stood unmoving, not breathing—not even blinking—while he kept his face impassive. Not only had he stolen the stone, but he had lied, and he had defied the *patrón*. To a man like Don Armando, death would be the only proper punishment.

"Nothing there," Jake said and handed the yellow band back to Niño, who slipped it over his head with the knot above his left ear. Only then did he dare breathe.

"Papá, maybe he's hidden it somewhere else," Lucia said almost in tears. "Tell Jake to flog him until he confesses. . . ."

"It's possible you lost it out by the river, Lucia *mía*," Miguel's words spilled out nervously. "I don't remember seeing it when you came back."

Don Armando grunted. "Miguel's right, child. That's probably exactly what happened. Come—don't cry now. Let's get back to the house. Your mother's waiting with refreshments." He put a hand on Lucia's shoulder. "Don't fret, my dear. I'll get you another cross—even prettier."

Before Don Armando strode out, he glared down at Niño. "I do not tolerate stealing," he growled. "It is wrong." He walked away, Lucia's hand in his. Tomás shuffled behind them, pausing briefly as he passed Niño. There was a half smile on his face—a smile that almost said, "I think you have it and I'm glad you got away with it."

As Miguel reached the door, Jake put an arm across his shoulders. "Good boy, Mike," he said, so low that only Niño and Miguel could hear.

Niño saw Miguel's face glow with pleasure before he drew away. "I do not like violence," he said coldly.

Jake's face, when he turned back to Niño, was twisted with some emotion Niño could not understand. He spoke gruffly, but with honest concern. "I reckon you know what would happen if you were caught with that stone."

"What would I want with a Catholic cross?"

Jake seemed amused at the remark, but his voice was stern as he said, "Get out to the cornfield—go on—git!"

While he ran past the chickens, the well, the building with a cross, and finally into the open fields, Niño thought about Jake. He was sure Jake suspected that he had found the cross and stolen the stone. Had he guessed that the stone was hidden in the knot of the headband? If so, then he had intentionally grabbed it there to keep the stone from falling out. Niño found it hard to believe that any white man would deliberately show a kindness to an Indian, when it could get him into serious trouble if the Indian were caught.

Niño shrugged. It didn't matter. Whether Jake had tried to help him or not, at least he'd avoided getting caught, so already the turquoise was working for him. He would be out of here soon.

# The Forked Tongue

A FEW DAYS after Jake started teaching the boys to swim,
there was much excitement at the hacienda. The *vaqueros*
had ridden out of the gate at the back wall, and there was
a general air of expectancy. No one told Niño what was
happening, and he did not ask.

"You won't go out in the fields this afternoon," Jake said
and hurried out of the front stables, heading to the big
house.

Niño was glad. It was miserable, tedious work, constantly hoeing in the fields, especially when none of the
delicious foods ever reached his mouth.

Just after Niño finished his scant mid-day meal, the back
gates opened again. Almost hidden by a rolling cloud of
dust, a herd of horses, driven in by the *vaqueros*, were
hustled toward the big corral at the far end of the pasture.

Niño stood by the stable door watching. Never had he
seen so many horses! To his surprise, when Jake returned
he did not send him out to water or feed the new animals.
In fact, he refused to even let him go near them. Until
now, it had been Niño's job to feed *all* the horses at the
hacienda. Yet today the *vaqueros* worked at the distant
corral and he was kept away.

Twice that day Niño questioned Jake about the new

herd. The first time Jake ignored him. The second time he cuffed him and said "Shut up."

Jake's gruff refusal to answer, when normally he was talkative, and the fact that only *vaqueros* were allowed near the corral, aroused Niño's curiosity. So when the evening meal was ended and his work was finished, he disappeared into the brush. In the fading daylight it was easy to make time while still covering any signs. For one thing, no one was in the fields—only the *vaqueros* near the corral were still working.

By dodging the circling *vaqueros*, Niño was able to get close enough to see the horses. There seemed to be nothing unusual—they were healthy, well-fed animals. Then he saw a small black one with a perfect crescent moon on its forehead and a round white dot on its shoulder. He would know that horse anywhere! How hard he had tried to get Brown Shirt to trade it to him.

The sight of the little horse brought such a sudden wave of homesickness that Niño's eyes filled. Quickly he blinked—a Navajo could never show emotion. Red Band had been firm on that point—if a man showed his feelings, another would know his weak point and could therefore defeat him. And although no one was around, the discipline was so deep-rooted that Niño's face became impassive.

At the same time his training at observation became acute, and he studied the horses. Many were unbranded and unshod—Indian ponies or wild range horses. But many wore steel shoes and had markings. In fact, one brand was repeated on many animals—U.S. He searched his memory, wondering where he'd seen that mark before. Then he knew! It was the same brand worn by the horses of the soldiers who had burned his home.

Slowly the suspicion grew in Niño's thoughts—stolen horses! The man in the eating place in Santa Fe had said many cavalry horses and Indian ponies were being stolen and sold in Mexico.

But surely Don Armando was not aware of the kind of herd he had just bought. Had not Niño heard him say to Miguel many times as they traveled, "Our family is an honorable one. Be proud you are the grandson of Don Ramon de Montilla"—this whenever Miguel would forget to behave in the cold, proud manner that so pleased the *patrón*.

Niño turned his gaze from the milling horses and gave a startled gasp. Crouched behind a bush a short distance away, his dark green clothes blending with the green of the bush, Tomás huddled with shoulders slumped even more than usual. His whole bearing was one of dejection.

Before Niño could melt back into the brush and get away unseen, Tomás turned his head, as though Niño's astonished glance had drawn him. His eyes, burning with disbelief and misery, stared at Niño, and in that brief glance Niño knew that Tomás, too, had recognized the horses as stolen, and in his heart he had accused his father of being involved.

For what seemed a long time their eyes locked, then Tomás looked away, his head going up proudly. Almost at once he snapped back, his face flushed with fury.

"Get away from here, you filthy Indian," he whispered

through tight lips. "How dare you sneak around where you're not allowed!"

Quickly, with his heart thumping in fear, Niño turned and disappeared into the brush. He had broken two very strict rules—he had shown himself in the presence of the *patrón's* son, and he had gone where he was forbidden. So great was his fear that he raced through the twilight, his only thought to hide in his room. Perhaps because Tomás did not like his father, he would not tell. It was a frail hope.

As he came dashing out of the brush back of the small building with the cross on top, he almost collided with Jake and several Mexican men who were talking. He knew immediately that his own face had shown guilt and accusation.

"Well?" Jake demanded, his tone cold and unfriendly. When Niño said nothing he added harshly. "Now you know."

Niño gulped. Unwittingly Jake had confirmed what Niño had tried to deny—the *patrón* knew the horses were stolen.

"I–I. . ." Niño started to explain, then he halted—stunned. Jake was also involved! It should not have mattered to him—Jake was a white man, therefore he could not be trusted. Niño's face became impassive and he stared unflinchingly into the blue eyes glaring angrily down at him. Not for anything would he let this man know it did matter to him—but only slightly, he told himself.

Jake cuffed him sharply again and again until Niño's

knees buckled and his ears rang, while the other men laughed. Evidently they were not aware why Jake was angry.

"Get to your room," Jake raged. "The next time you disobey a rule like this, I'll have Francisco flog you good!"

Scrambling to his feet, dodging another blow, Niño scurried across the grassless open area, past the well and stables, until he stumbled groggily into his room.

He ignored the two Utes who stared at him as he flopped down on his mat. As usual, he let fierce anger drive out his deeper disappointment. Then contempt replaced the anger—a man who did not live according to his beliefs was no man at all. Stealing was not wrong to an Indian. But to Don Armando it *was* wrong. Had he not said to Niño that he did not tolerate it? So Don Armando's tongue was forked—it was wrong for others to steal from him, but it was all right for him to take whatever he wanted. Before he fell asleep, he reluctantly decided that Jake was just like the *patrón*.

Early the following morning a band of Mexican riders came for the herd of horses, and although Niño could not see over the wall, he noticed the cloud of dust heading south toward Mexico.

As the days passed and nothing happened, Niño guessed Tomás was not going to tell his father. Maybe he didn't want to admit he had been there himself. But the amity between Niño and Jake was gone. Niño was sorry—more than he wanted to admit—and he had to remind himself frequently that this man was white, and therefore capable of such deceit.

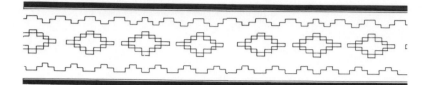

# A Debt is Paid

MIDSUMMER brought long days of heavy heat that made working in the fields almost unbearable for Niño and the other slaves. Yet even as he hoed the soil under the searing sun, he could not help sending out a small prayer of thanks to Father Sun who caused the fields to ripen. Though Niño was at heart a warrior, he had the love of growing things which was common to all Navajos.

About the time the sun's heat seemed almost too much to bear, strong hot winds came sweeping across the land, churning the dust into clouds that blotted out the walls and the hacienda, and driving everyone indoors until they passed.

They were followed by great black thunderheads that rolled down the mountains, bringing brilliant flashes of lightning, earthshaking thunder, and sometimes rain that began as great warm tears and ended as torrents of water.

The fields flourished and there was always plenty of corn, squash, and beans for the family in the big house. The lemon and peach trees bowed under their burdens of ripe fruit and even the big walnut tree near the hacienda was heavy with large brown nuts.

Niño's diet, however, never varied from its original beans and tortillas, although occasionally he found some chunks of meat thrown in on Sundays when the Padre reported that his catechism had been properly recited. There were times, too, when Consuela, Francisco's wife and the cook, managed to put some squash or corn in the bottom of his dish and cover it with the beans. Niño thought it strange for her to do this only for him, since she never spoke to him any more than to the other Indians. But sometimes he caught her looking at him in a way that reminded him of his mother just before she had said something like, "Eat, my son, eat it all so that you will grow big and strong."

Then he would wonder angrily how he could imagine this ugly Mexican woman—no taller than he and as wide as she was tall, with pitted skin and brown cow-like eyes—could remind him of Slender Woman.

Still, he ate everything Consuela put on his plate and always wished for more. Often at night he dreamed of his mother's thick mutton stew, rich with wild potatoes, onions, and tender young cactus shoots. He could see it and smell it, but he always awoke before he got any of it to his mouth.

Perhaps that is why, when he found himself alone one morning by the peach tree near the kitchen, he deliberately reached up and picked a peach from the lowest branch. For a moment he held it—soft and warm—in his hands, then greedily he sank his teeth into its sweet succulent flesh. All the memories of home and family seemed to be contained in the rich juice that ran down his

throat and dribbled onto his chin—the times New Found
Boy had boosted him up when they were both small so
that he could reach the best fruit—the strong sticky odor of
cooking sugar as his mother boiled the fruit for jam—the
way they had all laughed when Grandfather pretended to
have eaten too many peaches too fast on the day of the
gathering, and had gone around all the rest of the
afternoon clutching his stomach in mock suffering.

Suddenly he was aware of Francisco coming around a
corner of the kitchen shack. "Drop that peach!" Francisco
bellowed and ran toward him with his fists raised. The
force of the first blow sent the peach flying into the dirt.
The second sent Niño to the ground and he crouched,
waiting for the rest of the beating that he knew was due
him for daring to touch any food that was not given to him
at his meals.

But before the next blows could fall, a shout came from
the kitchen and Consuela exploded from the doorway
waving her short-handled broom and pouring forth such a
torrent of Spanish that he could only half understand it.
Seemingly from nowhere people appeared, slaves and
Mexicans, and dark-eyed children and dogs, all watching
curiously as Consuela berated her husband.

"Niño," he heard over and over again as she struck at
Francisco with the broom, and "little Niño," and "he's
growing," "he's hungry," "all this for one small
peach. . . ."

And again at the end, when her breath was gone and
Francisco had retreated a short distance, he heard her
croon, "Pobrecito—poor little one," while she looked down

at him so tenderly that he was ashamed that he had ever thought her ugly.

When Consuela saw that he was all right, she smiled. Then she trotted over to the half-eaten peach, brushed it off on her shirt and brought it back to him. "Eat it, Niño," she said.

"Yeah, you might as well," Jake drawled as he rose from his place under a nearby tree. Everyone spun around in surprise as he started toward them, and the other Indians backed away, knowing they should have been working. "But, mind you, leave the fruit alone after this, you hear?"

Francisco was making menacing noises again in his throat so Jake turned to him. "All right, Francisco, he's my business and I'll take care of him." He turned to those still staring curiously. "Go on—back to work."

Consuela backed away slowly, watching Jake, as if she expected to be scolded sternly for siding with a slave. Jake grinned at her and slid an arm across her plump shoulders. "You will spoil him. . . ."

"He is but a boy," Consuela said softly. "And boys get hungry."

"And you're a mother at heart." He patted her, then said in mock sternness, "Now get back to your kitchen while I deal with him."

Niño was just finishing the peach when Jake said, "For stealing that peach, you'll pull weeds out by the far wall every afternoon for the rest of the week."

Niño didn't care. He would remember the sweetness of that peach for a long time. And he would remember how Consuela had come to his aid because she was a mother and he was a boy and she didn't care at all that he was a Navajo.

By the third day his struggle with the weeds seemed like a losing battle. All up and down the long adobe wall the Indians were grumbling about the thorny desert shrubs. It was hard to see that they had made any headway at all. Niño was battling with a stubborn young mesquite when Jake appeared just inside the back entrance. He locked the gate and led his horse toward Niño.

"My horse went lame out there," he said. "Must have a stone wedged under his shoe." He hunted around in the pockets of his faded blue pants until he found a hoof pick. He bent over and lifted the horse's hind leg just as the bush Niño had been tugging on came loose. Niño lost his balance and tumbled backward while the bush flew out of his hand and sailed past the horse's head. It shied in fear and kicked both rear legs so violently that Jake was thrown against the wall where he fell limp beside a big clump of sage.

Niño got to his feet and grabbed the horse, murmuring to it soothingly. The he heard a noise—there was no mistaking that warning whirring sound—a rattlesnake! The horse panicked and shied as far away as it could with Niño holding the reins.

Jake shook his head and started to sit up, then he froze. The snake was only a foot or so from his face. It was coiled, head raised and weaving, ready to strike.

"Find a stick—bushwhack it—*pronto*," Jake ordered through stiff lips. He hardly seemed to breathe.

Niño came closer, feeling disdain for this white man's fear. He could not imagine a Navajo ever behaving thus.

"Get away—you crazy fool!" Jake whispered hoarsely, his eyes still riveted on the flat head so near his own.

Niño knew he could get rid of the snake, but he wasn't sure he wanted to. Feeling an overwhelming sense of power, he knew that the white man's life was in danger and that he, a Navajo, could decide whether the man lived or died. He wanted him dead, he told himself, as he wanted all white men dead.

But Jake wasn't all white men, or even just a white man. He was *the* white man who had healed his back and saved him from a brutal flogging, or maybe even death, when Lucia had lost the cross, and who had not told the *patrón* of his forbidden visit to the corral. Niño weighed these things against his hatred and the fact that Jake was a horse thief with Don Armando, then he made up his mind.

"Brother rattlesnake," he began and his words came in Navajo like a chant, "we're friends, you and I. You're helpful to my people, eating creatures that would destroy our crops. So we never disturb you." The snake turned its head slightly away from Jake as if charmed by Niño's soft-spoken words. "The gods put us both on the desert to live together in peace. This man did not mean to startle you. He was thrown beside your bush by accident. Now he's afraid because he doesn't know you as I do—as a brother."

Slowly Niño moved his hand past the snake's body and nudged it gently as he spoke. "There is room for us all.

The gods will smile on you as they smile on me, if we live in harmony."

Niño continued to talk, all the time guiding the snake away from Jake and toward another bush. Finally it lowered its head and slithered away, gliding over the dirt until it disappeared from sight.

"Whew! That was a close one!" Jake sat up, wiping the sweat from his face. Then he stared at Niño who was still kneeling in the dirt. "You *talked* it away!" he said as though he just realized what had happened.

Niño looked up. "Navajos do not kill unless it is necessary, and they never kill useful things, if they can help it."

Jake eyed him curiously, then grinned a lopsided sort of way. "Danged if I understand you, young'un. I know you'd hog-tie and brand me if you could, yet you saved my life. Why?"

Niño stood up. "Now my debt to you is paid. I owe you nothing."

"If you don't beat all!" Jake lifted his hat and scratched his bleached thatch of hair. "Independent little cuss, aren't you?"

The sudden grin that creased his face from his eyes to his jawbone was so infectious that, in spite of Niño's desire to remain aloof, he laughed. And it felt good—to be friends once again, to laugh with this man—equal—maybe even a little superior after today. It felt good—so good that he said to Jake in Navajo, "Maybe now you know that Navajos have five fingers!"

"What'd you say?"

Niño repeated it in Spanish.

Jake frowned, then as understanding came he grinned, although his blue eyes were serious. "Navajo—white man—same difference. I knew that all along."

Niño went back to pulling weeds. Somehow the sun had lost its blistering heat and the bushes seemed to come out easier. He touched the knot on his yellow headband. Ever since he'd found the turquoise, his life had been a little more tolerable at the hacienda. But he was still a captive, and he wanted to be a warrior instead.

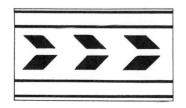

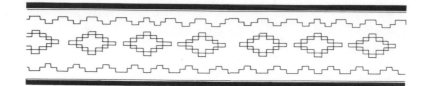

# A Day in the Orchard

IF ANYONE had told him those first months that two years later he would still be a captive at the hacienda, Niño would have been sick with despair. Yet twice the crisp, clear days of autumn had passed, twice the short months of bitter cold and rainy weather had come and yielded to spring. Now again it was early summer and he was still the Navajo Niño, thirteen years old and taller, stronger, wiser than Straight Arrow had been when he left Tsegi Canyon so long ago. His beloved deerskin moccasins had finally become so ragged he could no longer wear them, and, like his hated Ute roommates, he wore the clumsy hard shoes in winter. But most of the time in summer he went barefoot. He had outgrown the first faded blue shirt and tan pants, but he had been provided others that were different only because they were larger.

The yellow headband—constantly sweat-dampened—was ragged, but it was all he had in which to carry his precious piece of turquoise. He dared not hide it anywhere else, because he wanted the protection of it with him at all times.

Ever since their meeting near the herd of stolen horses, Tomás had ignored him completely. And at the passing of every four or five moons new herds would come, and they would go right out again the next day. Niño didn't have to go out and inspect them to know they were stolen—they were too sleek and well-fed to be mere range horses.

Don Armando cleverly kept a few of the Indian ponies and rangy-looking animals in his enclosed pasture and he even turned a few loose beyond the walls, luring them to stay close by putting out hay. That way, when visitors—cavalrymen, other Spaniards, Mexicans, or white men—stopped for a few days, he could show them his "herd," telling them there were many more grazing in the distant hills. He said his *vaqueros* were good fighters, well able to keep the Apaches from stealing his herds.

One morning a new herd arrived, but Niño tried to ignore it. For one thing, it reminded him that Jake was also involved. Since today he would not be working in the fields, Jake sent him to the peach orchard to clear away the heavy spring growth of weeds. Ever since the day he'd stolen the peach, Jake would never let him go near the orchard. That's why he had been surprised at first when Jake ordered him there today, but now he understood. There was no fruit—only delicately scented, pale pink blossoms.

Hoe in hand, he headed to the far end, then halted. Strains of music came to him and he saw Tomás sitting under a tree, strumming a guitar while he sang a song of such haunting sadness that Niño felt the same pity he'd known before. He knew Don Armando so violently disliked the "weakness" of his music-loving son that Tomás had to go to the far corners of the hacienda to play when Don Armando was home.

Niño hesitated. He was forbidden to go near the Spanish boy, yet Jake had been more definite than usual in his orders today. "You start at the far end and work this way. If you disobey me, I'll wallop you good—understand?"

Mimicking Jake's habit, he shrugged. "Flogging, walloping—same difference," he thought and walked over near Tomás to begin cutting out the weeds.

"Get away from here," Tomás snapped peevishly. Like Niño, Tomás had grown, too, even faster. He was still slender and pale skinned, but now he towered a whole head above Niño. Today he wore dark blue pants with a shirt of shiny blue cloth and sleeves that were very full and gathered at the wrist.

"I cannot," Niño replied, not looking at Tomás as he chopped the roots. "Jake ordered me here."

Tomás grunted and went back to strumming his guitar. Niño tried to ignore him, but the music fascinated him. It was so different from the Navajo chants he loved, yet the way Tomás sang, it was beautiful. The words, however, were sad. It was about a man who wanted something very badly and couldn't have it, and was slowly dying of heartbreak. Niño wondered what sort of sickness that was. After a while the music stopped.

Before he was aware he'd spoken, Niño stammered, "Your—your kind of singing—it is beautiful." Then he chopped frantically, horrified that he had even dared to speak.

"Do you like music?" Tomás asked.

Still Niño looked at his work. "I hear music when the drops of water skip over the pebbles in the stream, when the birds sing of their joy, and when the soft wind dances through the leaves of the tree. Even the loud voice of thunder is music and the howling of the coyote or the cooing of the dove is like a song. There is music everywhere in the heart of a Navajo." To his surprise, Niño realized he had stopped hoeing and was facing Tomás. But once he had begun to talk of the things of nature—so long hidden inside him—he could not stop the flow of words.

Instead of being angry, Tomás looked at him in surprise. "*You* hear those things, too?"

"Every Navajo hears them. We are brothers to the things of the earth."

"I hear them, too."

Before Niño could hold back the words he gasped, "But you are Spanish!"

Tomás laughed. "So I am—son of Don Armando, grandson of Don Ramon de Montilla, great grandson of the house of Montilla in Spain. My father never lets me forget. But I am also a lover of music." His face, dreamy and touched with wistfulness, suddenly became angry. "But I hate horses. I hate what my father does. I will not be like him."

Stunned, Niño dared not agree. So he merely stared at Tomás, his hoe dangling from his idle hands.

"Do *you* know what he is doing?" Tomás demanded as if suddenly aware that Niño might not have known the horses were stolen.

Niño nodded and the doubt on Tomás' face disappeared.

Nothing more was said and, embarrassed at the look of shame that clouded Tomás' face, Niño went back to work. After a moment he blurted out the one question that had bothered him for two years.

"Jake—he knows, too. Is that why he cannot leave here?"

Tomás put down his guitar. "No. Papá began dealing in . . ." he left the word unsaid, ". . . the summer before you came. At first, . . ." he shrugged, ". . . I didn't want to believe it. But. . . ." The resignation in his eyes said that he had been forced to accept it. "Oh, Jake knows," Tomás continued, picking up a peach blossom that had fallen, "but even before then he would not leave."

"He hates your—the *patrón*," Niño said and began hoeing half-heartedly. He did not dare look idle. There was always someone who might pass by.

"Ah yes—and my father despises him."

Niño didn't ask why, but his eyes silently conveyed the question.

Tomás shrugged. "I don't know, Indian. I think maybe—maybe Jake did something—something very wrong a long time ago."

"Wrong? Jake?" Niño could not accept this.

"Miguel and I talked of it many times when we were small boys . . ." his face hardened, "though we do not speak often to each other about anything anymore." The anger disappeared. "Papá dares not get rid of Jake, and Jake dares not leave." Tomás lowered his voice. "I know this, because I have heard them quarrel. Oh they get very angry! Very, very angry, and they swear at each other.

Papá has said, 'I will tell, and ruin everything for you.'
Then Jake would answer in a nasty way, 'And supposing *I*
tell—what then?' but always it ends with Papá hating Jake
and Jake hating Papá—but he stays."

Niño nodded, too stunned to speak.

"Miguel and I—we think somebody was killed," Tomás
continued, "maybe somebody important—Papá ordering it
and Jake doing it . . ."

"Or being *forced* to do it." Loyalty to his only friend
would not let Niño accept the thought that Jake would
obey such an order. He could be harsh and he had a nasty
temper, but surely he was not a killer.

Tomás jumped to his feet, his eyes shining. "That's it,
that's it—he was *forced* to!" His face glowed with relief, as
if glad to find a new thought that freed Jake from
something so horrible. "Jake is—he is . . ." he stammered,
visibly embarrassed at showing his affection for a lowly
cowboy, "fond of my br—of Miguel and me. And he is
good to you—all the children here—it is not in him to be
otherwise." Suddenly Tomás' face hardened, as if aware
that he had been confiding in an Indian, and angry that he
had done so.

"Get back to work," he snapped and threw his guitar
over his shoulder, striding off haughtily.

When Niño left his hoeing for the midday meal, Jake
asked him how much he had done.

"Only to the middle of the orchard. The weeds have
deep roots and are hard. . . ."

"No matter. Juan can do it this afternoon. I need you in
the stables."

As Niño worked that afternoon shoveling manure, a suspicion slowly dawned on him. Had Jake deliberately sent him out there, knowing Tomás was in the orchard? Niño had been aware for a long time that Jake was truly concerned about Tomás and Miguel. They seemed almost strangers to each other these days, as Miguel became more and more the fancy *caballero* and a pride to the *patrón*, whereas Tomás fell lower in favor because of his lack of riding skill and his love of music.

Maybe Jake had decided that even an Indian boy as a friend to talk to was better than no friend at all for Tomás. Then Niño gave a wry smile. Jake would not have been so happy to throw them together if he had known their conversation was about him—as a possible killer!

# The Lessons

IT BECAME clear to Niño in the following weeks that Jake
had thought to bring him and Tomás together to become
friends, but he had not reckoned with the Spanish boy's
deep pride. After all, a son of the house of Montilla could
not associate with an Indian slave. In fact, Jake seemed to
find many chances for the two of them to be in the same
vicinity. But always Tomás spoke only arrogantly or not at
all.

Niño was sorry. For so long he'd had no one near his
age to talk to, since even the young Mexican boys had
little to do with him. And shocking as Tomás' disclosure
had been, it had reminded Niño of his days with New
Found Boy, when they had secrets and told exaggerated
stories of enemy raids.

One day in midsummer he and Jake were working
together in the far stables. One of the horses had torn its
flank on some thorns and Jake was rubbing it gently with
his salve. Niño's job was to exercise a big bay that had
pulled a leg muscle a few days earlier. Patiently he walked
it back and forth, breaking into a run finally, to see if the
exercise bothered the muscle.

"How's he doing?" Jake called from the stable doorway.

"All right, I guess," Niño answered. "But he should be ridden to see if the muscle's really healed."

"Then ride him."

Niño couldn't believe his ears. "Ride him?" he repeated stupidly. Indians were never allowed to ride the horses. It was a rule.

"That's what I said—ride him."

Niño asked no more questions, but grabbed the horse's mane and swung himself up. The horse was trotting by the time he was on its back.

With a shout of pure joy, Niño raced across the back pasture. There was a short halter rope around the bay's neck, but he didn't bother to hang on to it. He gripped the animal with his legs and let it go. The horse reached out, stretching every muscle in its pleasure at running free again. Niño knew exactly how the animal felt, and for a moment he could imagine himself outside the walls, no longer a slave but Straight Arrow, a Navajo warrior racing away after a raid on a Ute village.

As he turned to come back, he saw Don Armando and Tomás ride in the front gate. Although he could not be sure he had been seen, he quickly headed to the stable, dismounted and began to curry the horse. Almost at once Don Armando appeared in the stable yard, his face dark with anger. Niño hid as well as he could behind the big bay.

Jake gave Don Armando no time to speak. "I told the young'un to test the leg muscle on that bay," he said easily. "I wanted it to tote a lighter weight than mine first time out."

Don Armando quieted a little. "I don't like it. He might take a notion to head out that back gate."

Jake shook his head. "No chance. It's locked, and it's too high to jump." He turned to Tomás who had followed his father slowly. "How was the ride?"

Tomás shrugged. "Just a ride."

"He'd bounce around on a rocking horse if it went faster than a walk," Don Armando snorted.

Tomás muttered and Don Armando raised his eyes heavenward. "What did I ever do to deserve a son like this? To think that someday I'll have to leave my ranch to this—this musician." He looked disdainfully at Tomás. "He can't even stay seated in a saddle."

Tomás flushed in discomfort and glared at his father's back.

"Hugging a saddle's not what makes a rider," Jake said. "It's having a feel for the mount."

"Then *you* teach him that," Don Armando ordered. "I'm tired of trying."

Jake shook his head. "I couldn't do it. But Niño could teach him fine."

"That *Indian!*" Don Armando was shocked. "Never!"

"There's no critter on earth that can outride an Indian," Jake went on. "You know that. And you saw Niño a minute ago—no saddle, no reins. . . ."

"I don't want to ride," Tomás interrupted crossly. "I can always use a buckboard. . . ."

Don Armando sputtered wordlessly for a moment. "A buckboard!" Then his face hardened. "Have that Indian teach him to ride. And if he doesn't make a horseman out of him by the end of the summer, I'll see that he gets the thrashing of his life."

Don Armando wheeled his gelding around and rode off, bellowing an order at Tomás, who meekly followed, his face glum.

Niño came from behind the bay and glared at Jake. How could anyone teach that bag of bones to ride? How could *he* do it? A slave—worse, an Indian—without authority or position.

Jake smiled at him—a slow smile that started in his eyes and moved over his face until it was all piñon brown lines and creases and shining teeth. "Don't get your back up, Niño. You can teach that boy to ride. . . ."

Niño turned his back on him without a word, and his shoulders slumped. Now he had nothing to look forward to all summer but the beating that was waiting for him at the end of it. Then a brighter thought struck him—the end of the summer was two moons away and in the meantime he would ride often. And, who could tell, maybe his chance to escape would turn up before then.

The very next morning Tomás came slowly toward the far stable, dragging his feet through the dust. Although Don Armando had not liked the idea, Jake had insisted that the lessons take place as far from the house as possible—at the back pasture behind the pond—so that there would be no interruptions or distractions. He had also insisted that no one was to disturb the boys—not even Don Armando, himself.

Now Tomás sullenly ignored Jake's greeting and went to stand in front of Niño, legs apart and hands on his hips. "All right, teach me," he challenged.

Niño's hopes fell. It wasn't going to be easy to teach Tomás anything. He was too defiant, and besides, he didn't really want to learn.

"You can start on this roan—it's gentle," Niño said.

"I want to ride the bay."

Niño nodded. "All right." The bay was spirited, but if that's what Tomás wanted, he wasn't going to argue. "Then I will ride the roan. The best way to get the feel of a horse is to ride bareback," Niño went on. "I'll show you how to mount. . . ."

"I *know* how to mount."

"Not without a saddle, you don't."

Tomás' eyes narrowed and a look of arrogance, so like his father's, made his head rise. Then he shrugged. "Well, don't just stand there—show me."

Niño went to the roan and grabbed the mane with both hands, then leaped lightly into the air so that his right leg went over the roan's back. "Like that," he said. "Push with your feet and legs and pull with your arms at the same time."

Tomás walked to the bay who skittered sideways. He managed to get hold of its mane and clumsily tried to throw his body up. But he didn't make it. The bay shied and he landed in the dirt.

Niño's face was expressionless. "It takes a lot of arm muscle."

Tomás struggled again and again, but each time the bay danced away, while Niño watched impassively, trying to hide his amusement. Finally something in the slender boy's determination made him realize that Tomás was ashamed that a mere Indian could do something he couldn't, and he was not going to stop trying. Tomás would injure himself if he kept on this way and he, Niño, would suffer for it.

He nudged the roan closer and thumped the bay on its head with his knuckles. "Settle down, you mule-head," he ordered and was surprised to hear himself using Jake's expression without his knowing he was going to do it.

Immediately the bay stood still and this time Tomás managed to get his leg across the animal's back far enough to enable him to scramble into a position to ride.

"It takes practice," was Niño's only comment. "Now let him walk. Just sit loose and keep your knees against his body. Don't worry about the rest of you."

"I don't like the sweaty feeling, riding like this," Tomás muttered. "I want a saddle between me and this hide."

"Later."

"Now!" It was an order.

Niño considered his position. If he angered Tomás, he'd end up getting flogged. If he allowed Tomás to dictate what was to be done, the lessons would fail and he'd get flogged anyway. Not much of a choice.

"No saddle," he said.

While they glared at each other stubbornly, Miguel

appeared by the stable door. He was not as tall as Tomás, but handsome and rugged in his black, silver-trimmed suit that showed off his rangy frame. His eyes, still a pale brown, looked scornfully at Tomás. "You call that riding? You'll never learn. . . ."

Jake came up behind him. "Move on, Mike. No one is going to interfere. . . ."

"I can go anywhere I want," Miguel said arrogantly and his eyes dared Jake to do something about it.

He did. He put a big hand on Miguel's shoulder and forcibly turned him. "So you can, Mike—but I'm boss in my territory. Now git!"

Miguel met Jake's stern eyes, his own defiant, then he shrugged, as though what Tomás did was of no importance, and he strutted off—still the courting jaybird, Niño thought with amusement.

When the boys looked at each other again, the fire of battle was gone, and in its place was amusement and a suggestion of conspiracy. Tomás was laughing.

"No saddle!" was all he said, but Niño read the rest of his face, "I'll show him—I'll show them all!"

He knew that Tomás would learn to ride now because he had a purpose. But he'd learn Indian style, the one way that would enrage his father and Miguel.

That evening, in the fading twilight, Niño was walking past the building with the cross—the Padre called it a chapel—when he heard a call. "Indian!"

Niño halted and peered into the shadowy doorway. The voice was Miguel's, but he could never remember the Spaniard speaking directly to him before, and he wondered what trouble he would cause now. Still clear in his mind was the disdain in Miguel's voice when he'd said to Tomás earlier, "You call that riding? You'll never learn."

"Did my brother ride well today?" Miguel asked, staying in the shadows.

"He will learn."

"Tomás, too, is proud," Miguel continued. "To learn from an Indian is—is. . . ."

"A thing of shame?" Coldly Niño finished the sentence.

"Today at the stable, I said he would not learn. But now he will—to show me I am wrong."

"You—you did that with a purpose?" Niño asked in disbelief. And before he could stop the next word, he asked it. "Why?"

"It is wrong that my father should compare us. Now he will be pleased with Tomás."

Niño nodded in surprise. He turned to go when Miguel spoke again, this time his voice only a whisper in the dark. "Teach him well, Indian. I do not want you to be flogged."

Niño walked slowly across the open area and paused at the well for a drink of water. His mind was confused. He had thought Miguel concerned only with himself. Yet tonight he had said he wanted Tomás to be accepted by Don Armando. And, strangest of all, he had been concerned lest Niño be flogged!

Truly these two Spanish boys were hard to understand. But he knew that although he did not like them, neither did he hate them as before.

# A Secret Disclosed

THREE DAYS a week Tomás came for his lesson. Slowly he developed enough power in his arm muscles to mount without the help of stirrups. And he learned to ride a trot without bouncing about like a sack of meal. At first Niño let him use reins, but as the weeks passed, Tomás was able to ride with nothing but the pressure of his legs to guide the horse.

One day when the lesson was finished, Niño went about his usual business of walking the horses to cool them before he brushed them down and cleaned their stalls.

"Good lesson?" Jake called from the far corner of the yard where he was shoeing a horse.

Niño shook his head. It had not been a good lesson at all—nothing had gone right. Now Tomás leaned against one of the stalls, whittling a sharp point on the end of a long pole. The corners of his mouth were turned down, and when he looked at Niño currying the bay, his eyes narrowed speculatively.

Niño tried to ignore him. He was used to these moods by now and whenever Tomás was sullen, Niño tried to stay away from him. But today Tomás wasn't going to let him alone.

"Why don't you get rid of that dumb knot of hair?" he asked offensively.

"Because I like it." Niño did not look at him.

Tomás poked the bay with the pole and it stomped around the stall, snorting with annoyance.

"Oh, go away," Niño muttered. "You act like a child."

"You can't talk to me like that, you—you stinking Indian!" Tomás raised his voice threateningly.

Niño met his angry gaze. Everything in him urged him to tangle with Tomás—his fierce Navajo pride—the warrior blood that ran hot in his veins—and his shoulders tensed. But he made no move and they glared at one another in silence.

"Get that horse brushed," Jake called sharply.

Niño turned back to his work.

Suddenly the long pole touched his head and flipped the ragged yellow headband to the ground where it lay between them. Niño spun around in fury and reached for it just as Tomás bent down and snatched it up.

"Give it to me," Niño demanded, catching an end of it in his fingers.

They both pulled and the rotting cloth came apart in shreds, letting the turquoise fall onto the dirt floor. In frozen dread, Niño watched Tomás. It was so quiet that even Jake paused in his work and walked over to see what was going on. He, too, stared silently at the turquoise.

Finally Tomás stooped and picked it up, holding it in his open palm while a slow smile lighted his face. "I

always thought you knew what happened to that cross."
Niño said nothing. "Did you know he had it?" Tomás
asked Jake.

"I figured maybe he did—but I couldn't find it on him."

Tomás looked back at Niño. "You know if my father had
ever found this on you, he would have been angry enough
to kill you."

"I know."

"Then why did you risk your life for a piece of stone
that's worth so little?"

Niño indicated the small cross that Tomás wore on a
chain around his neck. "That cross has no great value
either, except in its meaning to you. The blue stone has
much meaning to a Navajo."

Tomás flipped the stone and Niño caught it just as they
heard the jingle of spurs. All three started guiltily. Niño
looked at the shredded cloth of his headband—there was
no possible way to use it any more.

"Here," Jake growled in an angry manner as Francisco
came in. "Put this on and get that sloppy hair out of your
eyes." He pulled off his own blue bandana and threw it at
Niño. Turning away, he said over his shoulder, "and get
back to work." He began talking to Francisco, drawing
him back out to where he had been working.

Niño made a rolled band and tied it around his head,
then slipped the stone into the knot and tightened it
securely. He looked defiantly at Tomás who was just about
to go out the door, but Tomás winked—and Niño relaxed.
It was all right!

In spite of the fact that Tomás continued to treat him

with elaborate condescension, Niño enjoyed the lessons. For one thing, it was the only chance he had to ride. For another, it wasn't really work—it was play. When they were both racing across the back pasture, he could almost imagine he was once more in Tsegi Canyon with New Found Boy beside him.

One day as they returned to the stables, Niño saw Jake watching them with that wide grin on his weathered face. Then he knew that what he had long suspected was true—Jake was still working to get them together, hoping they'd become friends. But there was no way this could happen. Tomás was the proud son of the *patrón*—Niño was the lowly slave. Neither could forget that.

Today, while Niño walked and brushed the two horses, Tomás waited around and watched him work. It was not unusual for him to stay, but when he did, he rarely spoke. This time he leaned against a post and looked thoughtfully at Niño.

"How can you stand that smell?" he asked.

"I don't have any choice. Anyway, to me, horses smell natural and good—and clean."

Niño could see Tomás considering his answer. Then he asked in a voice so low that Niño had to strain to hear it. "How does it feel to be a slave?"

Niño's head snapped up as a hateful retort came to his lips. Tomás had often taunted him about being an Indian, but something in his present quiet—almost embarrassed—expression made Niño realize that for once Tomás was seeing him as another human being who might have feelings. So he merely said, "I hope you never have to know," and went on shoveling out the stall.

"Because the work is so hard? Or because you get beaten so often?"

"Neither. My father worked me harder than Jake does. And a flogging only hurts for a little while."

"Then why?"

Niño made no reply because he did not know how to say what he felt to this rich man's son. If he said it was degrading to be treated like a slave without religion or culture, when in fact he was one of the proud and mighty Navajo tribe—could Tomás understand? If he said it was insulting to be considered inferior, on a level only with animals—would Tomás laugh? He could not yet tell, and so he said nothing.

Tomás did not insist further. Instead he said, "Tell me about your father. When he worked you so hard, was he mean to you?"

Niño's shovel paused. He didn't want to talk about Red Band. It was not the Indian way to talk about the dead, but he felt he had to answer. "My father was never mean. He is dead now. There's nothing to tell."

It wasn't enough. Niño could see that if he wanted Tomás to continue thinking of him as a person, he had to say something about his life before he came to the hacienda. Tomás had to see him as someone apart from Niño, Don Armando's slave. So he went on stiffly.

"My mother is still alive—at least she was when I was taken from our canyon. She wove the blanket I wore when

I came here. And I have a sister. She is not like *Señorita*
Lucia. She's quiet. I have a brother, too—who loves the
sheep. We used to hunt and play together." It was hard to
talk of his family. Abruptly he put down his shovel and
rolled the wheelbarrow out to the dump pile. When he
returned, Tomás was still there.

"Is that all your family?"

"No, there's grandfather, too. He's old and he doesn't
hunt or go on raids any more. He used to stay at home
and teach us the legends of our people." Niño looked at
the purple mountain tops visible over the wall, hazy in the
distance. "We lived in a round hogan in a canyon with
cliffs so high they seemed to touch the clouds. And we
had peach trees—enough for many, many people to eat as
much as we wanted when they were ripe. . . ." His voice
trailed off and he began again to work with his shovel.

The jingle of spurs snapped the fine thread of communi-
cation they had spun between them, and they moved
apart. When Francisco entered, Niño was busy on the
next stall and Tomás was stroking a horse two stalls away.

"Well, here you are," Francisco said impatiently. "Come
along, your papá is waiting for you."

Niño worked on steadily and his heart felt lighter than it
had in a long time. Talking to Tomás had made his family
more alive to him than they had been in many seasons,
and less like something he had made up to comfort
himself with before he went to sleep at night. He did not
exactly like Tomás, but he thought that he understood
him. At least he understood his loneliness because it was
something they both shared.

That night it rained. Water poured from the sky in wind-whipped sheets, and lightning flung its chains around the heavens while thunder rumbled and grumbled its way not far behind.

The next morning Niño awakened to a clean and sparkling world. The air was cool and crystal clear without a mote of dust or a hint of moisture. The doves that abounded in the desert land cooed so loudly that their noise was a continual throbbing sound. Everywhere the people seemed happy. From every building came the sound of singing and humming as the Mexicans worked, grateful for the cooling of the air. Only the Indians could not sing. But in his heart Niño heard the music of the earth and he said a prayer of thanks to Changing Woman for her goodness in sending so much.

He hauled water and fed the horses and had his breakfast, impatient for the moment when he could mount the roan and be off with Tomás. By the time Tomás arrived for his lesson, the horses were ready and waiting at the hitching rail. It had been Niño's custom all these weeks to say nothing until Tomás spoke first to him. But today he could not contain the pleasure of his heart in this lovely morning, and so he spoke.

"Good morning," he said eagerly.

Tomás did not even look at him. "Hold this," he ordered brusquely, shoving something tied in a blue bandana into Niño's hands. He slipped the halter from the bay and swung easily up onto its back. Then he held out his hand for the bandana.

Niño's pleasure in the day was stained. He, too,

mounted and dug his heels into the horse's sides. Tomás caught up to him and side by side they raced to the far corner of the hacienda where the big cottonwoods spread their branches in welcome and the heart-shaped leaves shone washed-green in the sun.

When they could go no further, they sat resting for a moment and Tomás untied the bandana. Inside, Niño could see four golden-ripe peaches. Tomás took two and held them out to him.

"Here," he said. "For you."

Niño's mouth watered but he shook his head. "I do not want them."

Tomás was amazed. "But why?"

"I want nothing from you."

"But I do not understand—yesterday. . . ."

"Yes, yesterday we talked. But today—this morning—when I spoke. . . ." Niño watched furiously as Tomás smiled and then laughed out loud. He made a move to spur his horse away, but Tomás put out a restraining hand.

"Wait," he said and now he was serious. "Francisco was there, behind the stable—waiting and listening. Did you not see him?"

Niño shook his head.

"I thought not. It is because of my father—he does not want. . . ." he looked uneasy. "How can I tell you without saying it? He does not want me to be friendly with an Indian—especially you."

Niño had to smile because he was not surprised. "And you—how do you feel?"

Tomás looked away. "I used to think as my father—

maybe I still do—about *other* Indians. But about you," he looked now straight at Niño, "I think of you as my friend."

Niño snatched the peaches and wolfed them down while Tomás ate his more slowly. It was not the Indian way to express gratitude for a gift except by showing enjoyment. So Niño said nothing until he finished. Then he spoke from his heart.

"The peaches are twice sweet. They are like honey in my mouth and they remind me of my home."

Tomás was satisfied. "Someday I hope you will see it again—your home and your family, the cliffs that go up to the clouds, and the peach trees."

"The peach trees are gone, but I will see the rest —someday. I have sworn it!"

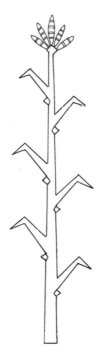

# The Quarrel

EVERY FEW months throughout the year, Don Armando rode north to Santa Fe and always he took Miguel with him. Sometimes Tomás had gone too, reluctantly. More and more Miguel was becoming like Don Armando, proud and haughty, and wherever the *patrón* rode, Miguel went along, riding with all the skill of a *caballero*.

One summer morning Don Armando, Miguel, and Francisco rode out the front gate on their way to Santa Fe. As soon as they were gone, Tomás hurried to the stables.

"It's time for our lesson," he said, his eyes bright.

Jake nodded and Niño hung up his shovel and got the horses. Soon the boys raced to the distant pasture, passing the few range animals Don Armando kept as a foil.

The lesson did not go well, however. Tomás seemed to have something else on his mind. And besides, the day was very hot. Even the horses didn't want to run. Tomás' blue striped shirt was sweat-soaked and Niño's body, naked to the waist, glistened wetly.

"You have taught me," Tomás said as they trotted side

by side in the narrow shade of the high adobe wall. "Now
I will teach you."

"*You* will teach me?" Niño could not imagine what this
boy could teach him.

"You'll see." Tomás heeled the bay and raced off with
Niño right behind him. How well he rides now, Niño
thought with pride. In a short while Tomás reined in
beside the pond.

"Take off your pants," he exclaimed. "You will learn to
swim." Niño looked around in panic. To laugh and play
while riding was tolerated, it was part of the lesson. Don
Armando did not like it, but he could accept it. But
swimming! Niño shivered, thinking of all the terrible
things that could happen to him if it were found out.

"Take them off. It is an order!" Tomás said in a voice
much like his father's.

Reluctantly Niño stepped out of the tan pants and
Tomás pushed him into the water before he jumped in
himself. Niño relaxed and enjoyed the refreshing coolness
on his hot skin. Maybe he would be flogged, but for now
he would have fun.

His hair got wet and the big knot felt heavy on his
neck. Fearful that he might lose the turquoise, he put the
headband on the ground by his pants.

They splashed, they played, and Tomás gave orders. But
no matter how hard Niño tried, he could not dog-paddle.
He could not float. He couldn't even stop swallowing
enormous gulps of pond water.

"Why must I swim?" he asked, sputtering as he came
up to the surface.

"Because if someday you get away, you might have to cross the Rio Grande. That is why Jake taught us."

Niño felt a rush of affection for this boy who was trying to help him be free someday. But he still could not learn.

"I'm not a fish," he joked finally.

"You're just a dumb Indian," Tomás replied, and Niño realized how close their friendship had become. Tomás' remark carried no intended insult and Niño did not object to it.

They waded out and put on their clothes, then while Niño untied his hair, formed a new knot and bound it, Tomás watched him.

"If you were free, would you go back to your canyon and tend sheep?" he asked.

Niño's head rose proudly. "I am a warrior."

Tomás gave a short laugh. "All you Indians are warlike," he said drily. "Why don't you try to live in peace?"

Niño's mouth tightened into a firm, angry line, but as he fought to keep from showing his fury, he realized Tomás was not meaning to be insulting. He was merely repeating what all white men believed—that the Indian alone was at fault.

"In days long ago, we lived in peace with all men," he said softly.

"Then why are you all so savage now?"

"The white man makes us so."

Tomás scowled. "How?"

"He steals our land. Ever since the white man came to this land, he has stolen whatever he wanted."

"But you don't need it all," Tomás snapped indignantly.

Niño looked pityingly at this Spanish boy who lived on land stolen from the Apaches. In time past, Don Armando had wanted it and his government had given it to him, ignoring the fact that it belonged to the red man. Yet he could not understand why the "savages" fought so brutally to get their land back.

"If a red man said you did not need this far pasture, would you let him have it just because he asks for it?" Niño asked.

"Of course not!"

Niño smiled, but said nothing. And in the silence he saw the expression on his friend's face change, as though suddenly Tomás had realized that maybe the white man was wrong—at least a little. And he knew, also, as he watched Tomás study him, that what Jake had strived for had finally come to pass—the wall of pride between Indian and Spaniard had fallen and they truly were friends now.

"Your brother—the one who likes sheep—did you like him?" Tomás asked after a long pause.

"Yes."

"Was he older or younger?"

"The same age."

"A twin!" Tomás looked surprised.

Niño smiled. "No, he was a Ute. My father captured him in a raid and brought him home. He was but a small baby then."

Tomás' dark eyes widened. "You—you had a—a slave!"

Niño put the blue headband over his still-damp hair. "No. A brother. He was never a slave, but was equal with me. We loved him."

Tomás looked across the pond at two hawks wheeling and dipping in the blue sky. His face was thoughtful. "Like our family—in a way. Miguel is not my brother."

"I know." Immediately Niño regretted his words. How could he explain he had listened while the two boys swam with Jake?

But Tomás—his thoughts far away—did not notice. "His mother, Catarina, was my father's sister. She lived in Mexico." There was a pause. "I was told her husband died and she didn't want to stay with Don Ramon. . . ." Tomás glanced at Niño. "That was her father." He looked out across the water again, idly letting dirt slip through his long fingers. "She was very unhappy and decided to come up here and stay with Papá until her baby came. She died when Miguel was born."

Tomás faced Niño again, eyes bleak. "But my Papá is not like your Papá. I was already born, but he favored this new one. We are not equal."

"Why do you work so hard to displease your father?" Niño asked, not knowing what he was expected to say. "Maybe he would not show favor to. . . ."

"Because I cannot please him no matter what I do." There was a silence, then Tomás asked, "Your father—was he pleased with you?"

Niño nodded, stiff as always when he spoke of Red Band.

Tomás' face was bleak. "My father despises me."

"I think it is just that he doesn't understand." Niño felt embarrassed by Tomás' frankness.

"No, he despises me. Does it ever happen so among your people?"

"Sometimes it cannot be helped if the father is a warrior and the son is a coward."

"I am not a coward," Tomás said with dignity. "But I am not a *caballero* or a—a man of action, like my father—like Miguel." He looked curiously at Niño. "What does a father do who has such a son among your people?"

"Sometimes he tries to change his son. But when this fails—and it almost always does—he sends him to an uncle or an older brother who will help him be whatever he is better suited to be—a keeper of the sheep perhaps, or a maker of tools."

"I would like only to make music," Tomás said dreamily.

Not knowing what to say, Niño rose and went to his horse. Silently they rode back to the stables.

For many days the two of them went to the pond after riding lessons. Tomás had reminded Niño that his father, Miguel, and Francisco were gone, and no one else ever came out so far from the house. For one thing, Jake saw to it that the *vaqueros* were kept busy elsewhere. Although Tomás was a good—if impatient—teacher, Niño did not learn to swim. But they did have fun.

One cloudy day they finished their ride and their romping in the water and rode toward the stables. They were still in the brush when they heard voices—loud and very angry voices. Don Armando and Jake!

"I—I did not expect him back today," Tomás gasped fearfully.

The boys paused, hidden behind bushes. Niño could see the two men in the stable yard, facing each other like fighting cocks.

". . . you can't bring back the dead," Don Armando was storming.

"No, but if you don't change what you're doing," Jake raged, "I'll—I'll. . . ."

"You'll what?" Don Armando gave a nasty taunting laugh. "Kill me?"

It was Jake's turn to laugh in mockery. "Not directly. But you know what I'll do."

"You wouldn't dare!" Don Armando sputtered. "You wouldn't dare, you—you common, shabby cowboy!" Again he laughed harshly. "You would ruin everything—including yourself. The soul of the dead would come back to mock you. No Jake—you'll stay here and suffer. It's your penalty for what you did."

Jake shoved a finger at Don Armando's face. "I did no wrong, but you. . . ."

"You did a great wrong!" Don Armando shouted, shoving aside Jake's threatening hand. He spun on his heel and stomped off, calling over his shoulder, "And you'll live with it the rest of your life. I'll see to that!" Then he was gone.

Wide-eyed, Tomás and Niño stared speechless at each other. This was not a game of pretend. Jake had really done something very bad.

"It—it is as I said," Tomás finally said shakily. "A great wrong—it can only be a killing."

"The *patrón*—he said the soul of the dead would come back." Niño shivered. It was just such evil spirits that he feared when confronted with *chindi*.

They waited until they were both calmer, then rode

slowly to the stable. Timidly Niño glanced at Jake's face, which was dark with rage. Gone were any signs of laugh wrinkles or of eyes bright with amusement.

"The *patrón* is looking for you," he told Tomás bluntly. "Go on—git!" He glanced at Niño's wet hair. "I didn't give you permission to swim," he snapped and cuffed him. "Clean up that stable. It's a mess."

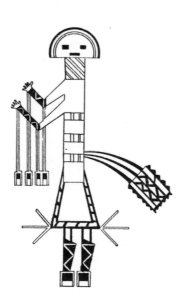

# Tomás Rides

SUMMER drew to a close and soon, Niño knew, Don Armando would demand to see the results of the lessons and he had still not persuaded Tomás to use a saddle. Even more than the threat of a flogging, he was sad because he felt he had betrayed Miguel's trust in him. And he was surprised to realize that this bothered him. While still out in the pasture one morning, when lessons were done, Niño made one last attempt to get Tomás to ride in the proper *caballero* manner.

"You ride that bay like an Indian. Even I could not do better." He saw Tomás flush with pride at the praise. "But to your father that same truth will be an insult. And I will be flogged."

Tomás looked stricken. "I did not think of that, Niño—truly I did not. Now it is too late! Only this morning my father told me that the lessons are finished and I must be ready to show him what I can do."

The lessons were finished! Niño hardly heard the rest of the sentence. There would be no more riding together—no more talking together under the cottonwoods. . . .

Glumly the two boys rode back to the stables where

Francisco was clattering about the yard cooling down his own horse and Jake was doctoring a colicky foal inside. Tomás dismounted and while he tied his big bay to the hitching rail, he said softly to Niño, "Thank you, *amigo*. I wish you well!"

Niño gave no sign that he had heard. He went about his business exactly as he had always done, although his heart was heavy and his steps dragged. He had just led the roan to the farthest stall when he heard Don Armando call out.

Jake stood up beside the foal. "In here," he said gruffly. Since the day of the last quarrel, Jake had been very quick of temper, as Niño's bruises affirmed.

Don Armando strode into the stable. "I have made arrangements with a big rancher in Texas to buy a herd of range horses," he said, drumming his fingers on a stall rail. "I'm planning to build up my herd again, so I don't have to . . ." He paused, clearing his throat.

"But the Indians. . . ." Jake said, his manner immediately businesslike, as if in matters of horses and hacienda business, he put aside personal animosities. "Won't they steal them again? Or do you plan to keep them all behind the walls? The grazing would soon. . . ."

"Since the government hauled all those savages off to reservations like Bosque Redondo, we haven't had any trouble," Don Armando said, pacing back and forth, his shiny boots kicking at the dust. "So we'll start by putting a good-sized herd, mostly mares, out on the range to multiply." He grinned, pounding a fist into the palm of the other hand. "We're back in business, Jake."

"A business more to my liking," Jake agreed, and even

from his distant stall, peering out from between the slats, Niño could see the easing of tension in the rangy overseer.

"You're to go out and bring in the herd," Don Armando continued. "There should be ninety—maybe a hundred head. How soon can you go?"

"I'll hit the saddle in the morning." Jake rubbed his chin. "I'll need a helper or two. That's too many for one man to handle alone."

Don Armando nodded. "I'll leave the details to you," he said and headed back to the house.

Niño felt his head spin with excitement. Jake was going outside and he needed a helper! Who else could it be but him? Hadn't Jake said from the beginning that Niño was his waddy? And once outside the walls with so many horses to ride herd on, Jake would have his hands full—too full to keep close watch on an Indian boy who was more than ready to make a break for freedom.

All the rest of the day Niño worked feverishly, putting himself in Jake's sight as often and as obviously as he could. But Jake said nothing and Niño went to bed without knowing whether or not he was going. He lay restless on his sheepskin, listening to the fitful snoring of Esteban and Felipe and watching the play of the moonlight on the big wooden crucifix that hung on the wall over Esteban's bed.

"Pray to Jesus on the crucifix," the Padre had said. Then he added, "But if you pray for freedom, don't expect an answer. It is God's will for you to be here, and here you will stay. Simply pray to be a good Catholic. That's enough."

Niño had nothing against the man on the cross. He even admired him because he had been so kind to everyone he met. As a matter of fact, Niño was almost willing to believe in the Christian God, their Virgin Mary, their Jesus, and their saints. After all, what were a few more gods—he had so many already. But he was hesitant to accept this religion completely because it belonged to the white man and to the Mexican.

Tonight though, Niño figured he needed special help and he decided to leave nothing to chance. So he prayed to the man on the cross—not for freedom—but only to be allowed to go with Jake. Then he took the smooth turquoise from his headband and held it in his hands, running his fingers over it reverently while he prayed for protection and for the fulfillment of his dreams. When he put the stone back in its knot, he was relaxed and able to fall asleep.

The next morning he stood by the stable door and watched Jake ride out the back gate with Diego and Carlos. No amount of pleading had done any good. Jake was firm—Niño could not go.

"First chance you got you'd slip your hobbles," Jake had said. "I need someone I can depend on."

"You can depend on me," Niño assured him. "I used to round up horses for my father—I know how."

"I'm sure you do, Niño," Jake grinned, "but I'll be busier out there than a bear with three cubs and I can't waste time hunting a foxy young Indian with only one thing on his mind."

And that had been that. Now as Niño watched the gate close behind them, he felt overwhelmed with hopelessness. Would he never get out of here? He picked up his shovel and began to clean the stalls. He thought of the two Utes who shared his room. They tried to forget their Indian origin—they had become Catholics—they were obedient—they tried to be Mexican and even had Mexican names. But they were treated like Indians—as despised and scorned as if they still wore deerskins and warpaint.

His dark thoughts were interrupted by the arrival of Don Armando and his entire family, and Niño immediately disappeared behind some bales of hay. All the others were mounted except Tomás.

"Why must you ride only one special horse?" Don Armando was complaining. "Haven't you learned yet how to be able to handle any horse?"

"I have learned, Papá, but today I want to ride the bay."

"I don't think he can ride at all, Papá," Lucia taunted. "I think he's just wasted the whole summer with that horrid Indian boy."

"Hush, Lucia . . ." Tomás' mother leaned toward her son. "Why don't you show us what you've learned, dear?"

"Yes, show us . . ." Lucia dared him.

Miguel, as usual, said nothing, but sat aloof, watching the others with the cool haughtiness that was becoming so characteristic of him.

"Francisco," Don Armando's voice was sharp, "saddle the roan. My son will ride it."

"No, Papá," Tomás said stubbornly. "Today I wish to ride the bay. Francisco, get the bay. And forget the saddle."

"What do you mean—forget the saddle?" Don Armando demanded.

"I'll show you." Tomás turned to the bay Francisco was leading toward him.

Niño wished the ground would open up and swallow him, for Tomás had buried his hands in the horse's mane, but then he had failed to push with his legs and had practically clawed his way up on its back. It was almost as bad as his first day.

Lucia giggled. Don Armando snorted and Doña Teresa sighed. Miguel scowled.

"We'll go out by the back pasture," Tomás said, and slouching and bouncing along, he led the way.

When they were out of sight, Niño mounted the little roan and followed them, keeping well behind them and out of sight. Tying the roan in a cluster of brush where he knew they would not go, he edged his way to a big cottonwood tree and scrambled up into its branches so he could watch.

Tomás detached himself from the group sitting on their mounts in the shade of a tree. Each was dressed in elaborate finery, as Niño had seen them dress before, whenever the Mexican *vaqueros* would stage a small rodeo for the amusement of the *patrón* and his family. These

rodeos were gay affairs with much singing, games, plenty
of food, and the fancy riding and roping that showed off
the horsemanship of the *vaqueros*, each dressed in his
fanciest suit with embroidery, colorful sash, and hat
trimmed with silver bands. Those that owned silver-deco-
rated saddles, used them in the exhibition. Miguel often
took part in these rodeos, resplendent in elaborate
costumes, and of course, his saddle far outshone any of the
others. And, Niño was forced to admit, Miguel rode as
well as the best.

Only the Spaniards and the Mexicans were allowed to
these affairs. Niño and the other slaves could listen to the
gaiety and smell the food, while they ate their monotonous
diet of beans and tortillas, but they could see only by
finding a good hiding place with a view of the rodeo arena.

Today's riding exhibition, however, was a private one.
No doubt, Don Armando did not want to be embarrassed
before his *vaqueros* and their families if his only son
should prove to be a poor rider.

Tomás rode under Niño's tree, his long legs dangling
loosely and he was as shapeless as a lump of dough.

"You coyote," Niño muttered as Tomás passed beneath
him.

Tomás glanced up, then looked away immediately. He
was laughing as he turned his horse, then suddenly he
gave a curdling Indian yell. The bay charged ahead with
Tomás' heels drumming his ribs. Tomás let go of the
reins, leaving them loose on the horse's neck and pressed
his knees tight into the heaving sides. His own body was
almost motionless as horse and boy moved as one. Racing

across the pasture, he wheeled the horse around and came charging back.

As he passed his gaping audience, he snatched his sombrero from his head and threw it at his mother's feet. On the next pass he disappeared from their view, swinging his body to the right side of the horse as he gripped the withers with his left knee and pressed his right foot against the horse's body for balance. Only his legs and hips were visible to his family.

He raced to the end of the pasture, turned once more and sped toward them. Then, in a fluid movement, he swung down, still gripping the horse's neck with his arms, and when his heels touched the ground, he threw his legs up over the withers, so he was hanging under the animal's neck. With another bounce of his heels on the ground, he swung around and righted himself on the horse's back. As he neared them, he bent down, gripping the bay only with his legs, and snatched the hat from the ground. Then, with another earsplitting yell, he clapped the hat on his head and brought the horse to such a dead stop in front of them that it almost sat on its tail. Clouds of dust billowed around him. From the middle of it he looked at his father.

"That's the most undignified riding I've ever seen," Lucia exclaimed.

"If you call it riding," Don Armando added uncertainly. He seemed puzzled—not quite sure how to react to what he had just seen.

"It's Indian riding, Papá," Lucia insisted. "It's not proper!"

"It's Indian riding, all right," Miguel admitted, his voice warm with admiration. "But riding like I've never seen before. You've learned well, my brother." He turned to the *patrón*. "He was as much a part of that horse as the withers itself. The Indian has taught him not only to ride, but to love it." He looked at Tomás sweating on his horse. "Am I not right, Tomás?"

Tomás' face registered surprise at the unexpected praise from the usually haughty Miguel, and he merely nodded.

"Yes. . . ." It was clear that Don Armando, like his daughter, had been ready to ridicule such unorthodox riding, but he had been confounded by Miguel's high praise.

"I think Tomás rode beautifully!" his mother spoke up for the first time. "It was exciting to watch him." She gave a sly glance at Miguel. "No *caballero* I've ever seen could ride like that." She smiled warmly at her lanky son and Niño sensed a friction. Could it be that Don Armando favored Miguel, but Doña Teresa did not? "My sorrel is the fastest horse we have," she continued. "Would you race me?"

Niño saw a look of delighted surprise spread across Tomás' face, then he grinned back at his mother and took up the challenge. "Let's go."

The bay and the sorrel charged off. Doña Teresa used her crop, whipping the sorrel with a steady rain of blows, and it drew ahead of the bay, while Tomás kept his spurless heels pounding his horse's ribs. In moments they reached the end of the pasture and turned—the sorrel moving in a wide arc and the bay wheeling sharply to draw close to the lead. Slowly it gained on the sorrel and by the time Tomás halted in another sudden stop, he was three lengths ahead and the obvious winner.

Doña Teresa laughed breathlessly as she pushed a loose strand of hair back up under her silver-trimmed sombrero. "Tomás, I haven't enjoyed anything so much in years—thank you!"

"He does ride well," Don Armando conceded grudgingly.

In his leafy shelter, Niño sighed with relief. Maybe he wouldn't get a flogging after all.

"But Indian riding . . ." Lucia was saying, looking at her brother with resentment.

Niño was quick to see that Tomás was well aware of his sister's jealousy and pleased by it.

"Yes," said Don Armando. "That won't do at all. It's all right for an exhibition perhaps—or for a heathen Indian. But my son is a gentleman. I shall tell Jake to see that he rides like one!"

As they all started back to the stables, Tomás rode a little apart from the group so that he passed under Niño's tree. He raised his laughing face briefly, murmured "*Amigo*" and was gone.

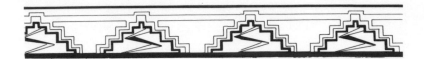

# Miguel

THE BRISK days of autumn brought a splash of color to the country of the Rio Grande in the land known as New Mexico, and the hacienda of Don Armando had its full share of golds, rusts, and browns. The big cottonwoods around the white house wore dresses of shimmering gold so brilliant that it put to shame the silver trappings of the Spaniards who lived here.

And these cottonwoods brought memories to Niño of the big trees in the canyon, their golden leaves making such a sharp, yet beautiful contrast to the deep red of the sandstone walls. Soon Changing Woman, now growing old again, would don her mantle of white for the winter.

It was on one of these cool mornings that Niño worked alone at the far stable while his thoughts were on Jake. How much more relaxed the man was now, since Don Armando was no longer dealing in stolen horses but had a good herd out beyond his walls. In watching Jake handle the new horses, Niño realized how much Jake really loved these animals. It was his whole life—this work. Oftentimes he'd talk to Niño as they worked, telling of experiences when he lived in Mexico. He had begun as a "waddy" roping and branding cattle, but had changed from cattle to horses because he preferred working with them. Niño yearned to ask him why he came to work for Don Armando, but a Navajo never asked such a personal question, so he said nothing. Jake was not required to work in the stables, but he did so because of his love of the animals.

He was so busy thinking about Jake that he did not hear anyone enter. So when he turned, shovel of manure in his hand, he almost spilled the contents on the shining boots of Miguel.

*"Perdón,"* he said automatically, backing away without looking up at Miguel, as was proper behavior for slaves. Quickly he returned to his work. He didn't know whether Miguel had left or not, but he dared not turn around to look. Therefore he was startled when after a long silence, Miguel spoke.

"You like Jake, don't you?"

Niño nodded, still working.

"He taught me to ride." Miguel's voice had a friendly sound to it, the same warmth Niño had noticed the day they arrived at the hacienda and Miguel spoke to Jake.

Niño didn't know if a reply was expected, but as the silence dragged on, he murmured, "Jake is a fine rider—he loves horses."

"So do I."

There was another long silence, broken only by the scraping sound of the shovel.

"Now you will teach me to ride—Indian style," Miguel said finally. It was an order.

Niño spun around, eyes wide. "Oh, no!"

"Because you don't want me to ride like Tomás, eh?"

"No—no. It's not that. But Don Armando, he . . ." Niño paused, not sure what to say. The *patrón* had not been too pleased about Tomás riding as an Indian. For Niño to teach such ways to the favored Miguel—it was unthinkable.

"He need not know." Niño shuffled his feet nervously. That made it even worse. "Tomorrow we meet out in the pasture," Miguel ordered. "Be there."

"B-but—Jake. . . ."

"I'll handle Jake. He'll do anything for Tomás and me. Remember—the pasture." He turned and walked out, leaving Niño staring after him in despair.

The next morning as he left the kitchen where he'd eaten his morning meal, Niño saw Miguel riding out of the front stables. He did not head for the pasture, but disappeared around one of the porch arcades of the house.

Evidently Miguel had already spoken to Jake, because when the overseer arrived at the far stables a short while later and saw Niño removing burrs from a horse's tail, he asked, "Are you using the bay or the roan?"

"T-the roan."

"Then get going." Niño mounted, but before he rode out, Jake called softly. "Do a good job, Niño. It means a lot to him."

Once out in the pasture, it didn't take Niño long to find out that Miguel was truly a good rider. With or without a saddle, he had a feel for his mount. And much to Niño's surprise, Miguel followed his instructions without question and with genuine good will—better even than Tomás had done. They rarely spoke, other than about how to ride, but as the days went by, he realized Miguel really did love horses.

Too bad he can't inherit the *patrón*'s hacienda, Niño thought. Tomás doesn't want it, but the house and all the horses will belong to him someday, anyway.

At first he had been reluctant to teach Miguel as much as he'd taught Tomás—feeling disloyal to his friend. But he soon realized Miguel's desire to learn was not so he could outshine Tomás, but because being able to ride the way Niño did made him feel more a part of the horse.

"We'd better end our lessons," Miguel said one morning as they rested in the shade. Whereas Niño and Tomás often sat close together, even leaning against the same tree trunk while they talked, Niño dared not be so free with Miguel. There was always that faint aloofness that reminded him he was only the Indian slave. Yet he learned to like Miguel, sensing a loneliness in the older boy.

At times he felt that Miguel was torn between two desires—to be a great *caballero*, exactly as Don Armando wanted him to be, yet at times to forget his proud heritage and just ride horses and be around them. Several times Niño had seen him watching the *vaqueros* at work with a sadness on his handsome face, as if Miguel wished that he, too, could be doing such strenuous work.

"Papá is beginning to suspect something," Miguel continued, "because I'm gone every morning. I tell him

I'm merely riding around the hacienda, inspecting things, but I think he believes I'm seeing Jake secretly."

"He does not like Jake," Niño said.

"No, he sure doesn't! Jake taught me to ride, he taught Tomás and me to swim, and he even taught me to play the mouth organ. . . ."

"The what?" Niño asked in surprise.

Miguel pulled something out from under his shirt, something slender and about as long as his hand that hung on a leather thong around his neck. It had a row of tiny holes along one edge. Miguel grinned, a smile warm and friendly. "This—it makes music." He put it to his mouth and blew.

Niño's eyes widened in surprise. Such strange music! Nothing like the guitars the Mexicans played, nor the big marimbas. Not even like the sad music Tomás played. This had a cheerful, happy sound.

"Jake was very good at it," Miguel continued when the lively song ended. "He taught me how, until Papá learned of it. He was furious! He forbid me ever to play it again, and he threw away every one he could find. Jake has never played one since."

Devilment danced in the golden eyes. "But Papá never found this one." Miguel's hand caressed it lovingly. "It was Jake's. He told me he'd had it since he was a young boy, and he gave it to me the Christmas before Papá forbade my playing."

"But the *patrón* loves music, as long as it is not Tomás who makes it." Niño had seen the *patrón* smiling and tapping his foot as others played.

"Ah yes, but he hates Jake more."

Niño said nothing. He dared not tell Miguel what he had learned from Tomás about the conversations between the two brothers when young boys, wondering what Jake had done. Nor did he wish to tell about overhearing the quarrel. He did not know this one, or trust him, as he knew and trusted Tomás.

"I am sure it is because of . . ." Miguel continued.

The loud cawing of a crow startled them and seemed to draw Miguel back from his brooding thoughts, reminding him he was speaking of personal matters to a mere slave. He rose proud and straight. "It's a matter for Papá and Jake. I cannot hate either. Let's go." He mounted and no more was said.

Niño missed the lessons. He even missed the lonely, quiet boy who loved horses. Too bad the lessons had been forced to end so soon, he thought, because although Miguel learned fast, there had not been enough time for him to practice the tricks Niño had taught him.

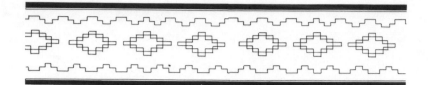

# Tomás' Gift

BETWEEN his thirteenth and fourteenth years, Niño grew three inches. He knew he was growing fast because nothing fit him. His shoulders burst the seams of his shirts and his pants had crept up almost to the calves of his legs. And he was able to look at Jake, eye to eye.

He envied Tomás who, for this whole year, had been living in Mexico City with an uncle, the brother of his mother. Before he had left he had managed to see Niño for a moment.

"I am going away," he said with great excitement, "thanks to you, Niño."

"To me?"

"Yes. I told my mother what you had said about your people—you remember, sending the son who could not please his father to an uncle or an older brother?"

Niño nodded.

"And my mother thought it was a very good idea." Tomás laughed. "She also thought it was a good idea to separate us, *amigo*—if we had got close enough to be talking of such things to each other."

144

Niño tried to smile at his friend. "I'm happy that you are to go," he said. "Will you be able to make your music there?"

Tomás shrugged. "I don't know. But my uncle is a professor at the university and I will study and learn. It will be better than here, I'm sure."

Niño did not know what a professor or a university was, but he could see that Tomás was delighted with his plan, so he nodded. Tomás put his hand on Niño's shoulder.

"You, too, will find your freedom someday. Of that I am sure. Every time I go to church, I will pray, *amigo*, that you find it soon."

That had been in the fall.

Now for the second time since Tomás had left, a flurry of snow lightly covered the ground and an icy wind cut through Niño's clothing like a knife. The soles of his shoes were worn through and his toes had broken out the front so his feet were always cold.

December brought Christmas. This was important to him only because it meant, for one day, slightly less work and a dinner that satisfied both his stomach and his appetite for something that tasted good.

He went to Mass where the warmth of the crowded bodies made him so sleepy that he knelt and rose during the service as in a dream.

Whatever Niño thought of Christmas as a religious celebration, he liked it as a fiesta. There was music in the air—music from the big house that came to him muffled and indistinct—and music from the Mexican workers' quarters, noisy, insistent, and clear. As he returned to his room after the evening meal, he heard children laugh with excitement and adults cry out in pleasure. Through the windows of the Mexican house nearest the slave quarters, he saw something Jake had said was a *piñata* hanging from the ceiling. It was a hollow paper donkey made of many colors—red, yellow, blue, and green—and as it swung around and around, small children, their eyes covered with a cloth, took turns trying to hit it with a long stick. When they succeeded, the donkey burst open and a shower of gifts fell to the floor for the children to gather and keep.

He could not help smiling as he watched, they were all so happy and excited. Then he noticed a little girl who sat alone in a corner looking shy and frightened. She reminded him of Timid One and he wondered why her father was not there to reassure her—as Red Band had so often reassured his sister. And again he felt the pangs of homesickness for the days when they had all gathered in joy and anticipation at a ceremonial sing, just as these children now were excited. How long, he wondered, had it been since he had sat around the campfire at night, listening to the tales of great warriors, dreaming of the day he would become one. And once again the fire burned bright in him. His day would come when he would return to his people and be a warrior, when he would be great among his own.

He felt a hand on his shoulder and, startled, he turned.

"Merry Christmas, *amigo!*"

"Tomás!" Niño gaped at his friend who stood before him, tall and straight, splendid in a close-fitting dark suit

elaborately trimmed with silver that shone even in the
pale light from the small house. Remembering the dusty,
slouching, uncertain boy who had come to him to learn
how to ride, Niño felt himself face to face with a stranger.
"You have changed," he said, "from a crow into an eagle!"

Tomás strutted proudly. "I have learned many things,"
he told Niño. "I can make music so beautiful that people
will pay to hear me! My uncle sees that I have
lessons—that I study."

A wide warm smile of joy spread across Niño's brown
face. "I am glad," he said simply. "And your father—he is
pleased?"

Tomás shrugged and for a moment Niño had a glimpse
of the boy who had stood at the gate that very first day.
"To him making music is an inferior thing. But he is
pleased, at least, that I can do it well."

Tomás grabbed Niño's arm. "Come, follow me. It is
much too cold out here and I have something to tell you."

Tomás led him past the corner of the big house and
onto the tiled porch. He opened a door into a room, but
Niño stood just off the porch, not moving. Never in all the
years he'd been here had he stepped foot in any part of
the big house. It was absolutely forbidden.

"Come," Tomás insisted. "No one will see. They are
more interested in the fiesta."

Trembling from dread as much as from the cold, Niño
crossed the tiles and entered the doorway. The room was
large, with so many lanterns that he blinked in the sudden
glare. The windows were covered with thick blue cloth,
and on the polished tile floor were rugs so thick that it

was like walking on sheep's wool after the shearing. But the nicest thing about the room was the warmth coming from a huge stone fireplace. Quickly Niño moved over to it and held out his cold hands. Even his icy exposed toes felt the warmth and began to tingle.

"Is this where your family sleeps?" he asked, thinking how comfortable it would be to lay down on the soft rugs and sleep near the fire.

"Only I sleep here. Everyone has his own room."

This was a surprise to Niño. In his hogan, everyone slept in the same round room, spreading out around the small fire in the center of the dirt floor.

Tomás sat down on a small wooden stool near the fireplace and Niño squatted in the position so comfortable to the Indians.

"I have learned something, *amigo*," Tomás said in a low voice and leaned forward. "I learned it from my uncle's family." A look of intensity made his dark eyes glow. "It is about Jake."

Tensing, not sure whether he wanted to hear it, Niño waited without speaking.

"It is a long story," Tomás continued, "and a sad one. It makes me love Jake more—and also Miguel."

Still Niño said nothing, remembering what Miguel had told him about the music he hung around his neck—music given to him by Jake.

"I will start at the beginning," Tomás went on. "Jake worked for our grandfather, Don Ramon de Montilla. He also played music—gay, happy music—and he was young— not as we know him—and colorful in the saddle. With his hair—yellow those days and not burned dry as we see it—and his blue eyes . . ." Tomás laughed. "The ladies thought him handsome—one lady in particular—the only daughter of the house." When Niño said nothing, Tomás continued. "One day, when Don Ramon was away—up here visiting his son, Don Armando—Jake and the daughter got married." Tomás paused, waiting, his eyes bright with expectancy.

Niño scowled. What did that have to do with anything? Then his eyes widened. The daughter of the house—Catarina—Miguel's mother!

"Yes," Tomás said, seeing that Niño understood. "Catarina was Miguel's mother, so Jake is his father!" The words were said almost with reverence, as though Tomás considered this almost an enviable thing. Then he continued his story. "Don Ramon was furious. But Catarina was happy and would not leave her Yanqui. Many months later Don Ramon sent Jake to a far-off place to get more horses. He was gone for six months. When he returned, Catarina was gone and no one would tell him she had left him a letter. It was destroyed. He nearly went mad with grief."

Niño's heart ached for Jake. "Where had she gone?"

"Up here, to Jake's country to have her baby—here at this hacienda."

"But Don Ernesto?" Niño asked, confused by the developments.

"There was never a Don Ernesto. Papá made up that name so everyone would think Miguel was of noble birth, and not the son of a. . . ." Tomás paused and Niño remembered Don Armando's words of rage ". . . you common shabby cowboy."

"It didn't take Jake long to find out where Catarina had gone. But already it was too late. She was dead and Papá had her baby. He would not give it to Jake."

"No wonder there is hate between them."

"Yes. Papá said he could give Miguel so much more than Jake," Tomás explained, "so Jake said he would stay on at this hacienda to see that Miguel was properly raised."

"Miguel—does he know?" Niño asked in an awed voice.

Tomás shook his head. "Oh, no. He thinks that the trouble between Papá and Jake in some way has to do with his father, Don Ernesto—who doesn't exist, of course." Tomás poked the fire. "That is why Papá will not send Miguel to Mexico. He knows he would learn the secret. That is why he did not want me to go. But my mother insisted."

Only the crackling fire disturbed the silence that followed. Niño remembered Jake calling Miguel "Mike" which he'd explained was the way the name was said in his country. And Jake teaching Miguel to ride and to swim—and to play his kind of music. No wonder Don Armando had been so angry. Jake wanted his son to do the things he loved, and Don Armando wanted him to be a *grandee*. And Miguel—he was caught in the middle, loving both men, and loving horses, not only as Don Armando loved them to buy and sell, but even more as Jake loved them, to be close to them.

Tomás rose and walked over to the table, then came

back to Niño. "I cannot stay longer," he said. My Papá—you understand?" And he held out his hand. "For you."

Niño removed the bright paper wrapping carefully, then opened the box that was inside. And there, on a soft bed of white, lay the most beautiful piece of turquoise he had ever seen. He looked at Tomás through eyes that were covered by a strange mist.

Tomás spoke hurriedly. "It is to help you get away. I thought a big stone would have more magic—more power—than the other."

Niño smiled.

"I wish I could do more," Tomás rushed on. "But I am, after all, the son of my father and I cannot betray him."

"It is all right. I understand." The warmth of the turquoise seemed to spread from the palm of Niño's hand through his whole body.

"*Adiós, amigo.* Don't ever despair—trust your god. . . ." Tomás opened the door and Niño moved silently out into the cold. He stood under the bright stars and, holding the warm stone in his hand, prayed to Turquoise Woman in wordless longing, "I am ready—now I am ready."

# The Bronc Buster

JUST at the time that Changing Woman was throwing aside her old age to become young again, Jake brought in a big herd of horses to be broken for a buyer who would come to pick them up in September. Most of them had been broken once before, but after a year on the open range they needed taming all over again.

Niño stood beside the corral rail, oblivious to the kicking, biting and squealing, and crooned softly to them.

"You'd make a first-rate bronc buster, Niño, if you'd only learn to use a saddle," Jake said.

Niño looked at him with disdain. "A Navajo doesn't need a chair on a horse to tame him."

Jake chuckled. "Reckon you've never broken a bronc, or you wouldn't talk like that."

"My father tamed horses without a saddle. I am the son of Red Band." His shoulders squared as he said the words.

"All right, son of Red Band, let's see you tame this one!" Jake roped a wild-eyed paint mare from the herd.

She was shying and bucking even before Niño got on her back and he never did get his knees tight to her sides.

A dozen times he sprawled in the dust when she bucked him off, and a dozen times he climbed back on. His backbone felt as though it had been rammed up into his head—his teeth nearly cut his tongue in two—and his eyes swam dizzily in their sockets. But he was determined that he would learn how to stay on these wild horses without a saddle, until they accepted his presence as inevitable.

It took three hard, bone-crunching, back-breaking days. But on the fourth day the mare trotted up to him and let him mount and ride with no more than a nervous quiver of her flesh. After that it was a small matter for Jake or one of the *vaqueros* to get her adjusted to a saddle again.

From then on it was Niño's job to help Jake break horses. It was painful and it was exhausting, but it was man's work and he was proud to be able to do it. It also meant that he was finally free of the task of hoeing the fields.

As the days passed, the trees feathered out in soft green leaves and the corn began to thrust pale, tender shoots above the ground. And everywhere in the trees and bushes, birds were building their nests.

"Another spring," thought Niño, "then another summer —it is too long. I have been in this place for four springs. Already I am fifteen years old." He fought down the despair he felt, reminding himself that he *would* be free—to fight and to lead his people.

Through the hot months of summer he rode the bay whenever he could, practicing all the things he needed to be able to do if he wanted to survive after his escape—how to hang suspended from its neck as it galloped across the pasture—how to disappear from view as Tomás had done—and how to leap on its back from behind.

In the middle of summer, Jake came out to watch Niño work with the horses. He sat on the corral rail and shoved his battered hat to the back of his head. "Hey, Niño, come here," he called.

Niño worked his way between the animals until he reached Jake.

"Got some news for you," Jake said, his face creased in its widest grin. "The government made a peace treaty with the Navajos sometime last winter. The Indians promised never to fight again, so they're free to go home to their land. This guy I was talking to said most of them had already gone from Bosque Redondo when. . . ."

Niño's dark eyes glowed. "Then my family could be back in Tsegi Canyon by now!"

"Maybe—if they're alive." Jake scratched his chin. "Seems like the redskins had a rough time at Bosque Redondo. Nearly half of them died of starvation. . . ."

"But the white man promised to feed them," Niño said tightly. "Does he always speak with forked tongue?"

"No, not always, Niño," Jake replied. "A lot of the white soldiers died, too, because they didn't get enough to eat. Crops weren't good—oh, you know, things like bugs eating them, storms flattening everything—problems nobody could control. It was a bad time for everybody. But all the Navajos who are left are back on the reservation—and that's where they have to stay."

"A Navajo wouldn't want to be anywhere else."

"Well, it seems a few of them have notions about

wandering all over the place, raising a ruckus, and when the soldiers catch them, they lock them up. Forget them, too." Jake grunted and went on talking as much to himself as to Niño. "Doesn't seem fair, somehow—but it's like this slavery thing. Slaves are illegal now in this country, yet the government sort of looks the other way when the slavery involves rich haciendas—and the slaves are Indians."

"Jake," Niño spoke in a voice tight with desperation, "Jake, can't you help me get out of here?"

Jake stirred uneasily and fingered the red scarf around his neck. "Niño, I'd sure like to. I really would. I don't cotton to this idea of slavery for anyone—never have. But . . ." He looked away, unable to meet Niño's pleading eyes. He jumped down from the corral rail, swearing softly under his breath.

Niño watched him go, his own face impassive, though within himself he was torn with emotions he couldn't control. To keep slaves, now, was wrong. Yet he was still a slave. And Jake, the only one here who could help him, would do nothing. Anger at Jake rose like a wild blaze until it was all he could feel. Yet under the fire was one small voice that said softly, "You know why he can't."

Ever since Tomás had told him the story of Jake, Niño had felt a strong love for this sunburned, straw-haired, rangy man. He was sure Jake stayed on here, hating Don Armando, so he could be near his son. And Don Armando would not send him away for fear he would take the boy.

Although Niño loved Jake for his sacrifice, he thought he was foolish. He should have stolen his son away and gone elsewhere. But this would be the way of Red

Band—not Jake, a white man. He seemed to be concerned with things like a fine home and something called schooling, whatever that was. Now that he thought about it, Niño remembered that many times, when Jake was talking of "Mike," he would say, "He has a fine life ahead of him," then he would add, as if to himself, "not like me, just a cowboy."

Jake dared not let Niño go free—this Niño knew very clearly—because Don Armando would learn of it and send Jake away. And if Jake would not leave, there would be serious trouble. Maybe even Miguel would learn the secret. And Niño knew Jake did not want this proud boy to learn that he was only the son of a "shabby cowboy."

But the thing that depressed Niño most—even more than the fact that Jake would not help him get free—was Jake's comment that the Indians had agreed never to fight again—an agreement they were forced to keep—if they wanted to live on their sacred land. After all his rigorous training, after all those years of hoping, now he could never be a warrior like Red Band. For a while he even lost all desire to get away from the hacienda. After all, a slave was all he was. Even if he escaped and returned to Tsegi Canyon, what would he do—tend sheep? Every inch of his lean muscular body tensed in rebellion at the thought and in his despair he understood a little of what Tomás had gone through, wanting to be one thing and forced to be another.

One morning, several weeks after his conversation with Jake, the buyer of the newly broken horses arrived with his crew. And Tomás came home for a short visit. Niño saw him from a distance, almost as tall now as his father, and walking straight beside him. Jake reported that Don Armando wanted Tomás and Miguel present at all the discussions about the horse deal and simply never let the two young men out of his sight.

Between breaking the last of the wild horses and taking care of all the feeding and watering, Niño had no time to care.

In the morning Jake came to the corral. "The buyer wants to leave tomorrow, Niño. Have the horses watered and fed so they can leave at sunup."

The stars were still out the next morning when Niño got up. There was a smell of fall in the air, he thought, and a smell of rain. It was unusually still and the atmosphere was threatening. He could see the soft glow of a lantern in the kitchen, which meant Consuela was getting breakfast ready for the men before they left.

Niño went first to the far stable to water the bay and lead him out of his stall. Then he rode to the distant corral where the newly broken horses waited to be released. When some of them neighed in recognition as he rode up, he was sorry that they would soon all be gone. He forked hay into the feeding bins and filled all the water troughs, stroking a soft nose here and patting a sleek rump there.

Below the clouds, the sky was brightening in the east by the time he was finished. And the wind was rising with the sun. When a group of horsemen rode toward him, he recognized Jake, Diego, Francisco, Miguel, and Don Armando. The others he did not know.

In the corral the horses pawed the ground, thunder growled in the distance, and a lively wind whipped gray clouds across the sky. Niño mounted his bay and moved away from the approaching men.

"All right, let's get them moving," Jake said to Diego, who opened the corral gate. "Open the back gate, too, Diego," Jake called. "Then we can drive them right on out."

The visiting cowboys rode back and forth trying to get the horses started, but the animals seemed reluctant to leave the protection of the corral. Niño saw Tomás gallop up to lend a hand, but when Miguel joined him, Don Armando called out in fury, "Let the *vaqueros* do that work. You come back here." Miguel, however, his whole body leaning forward with eagerness, seemed not to hear.

"Hey, Niño," Jake bellowed. "Get in the back of that corral and shove those critters out. But do it easy-like— don't panic them. They're touchy this morning."

Niño rode through the corral opening and edged his way to the very back of the herd. He yelled and nudged the horses, trying to push them toward the gate.

"Come on—come on," Jake cried. "We don't have all day!"

There was a sudden clap of thunder and a big black gelding squealed in fright and kicked out both hind legs. He struck the mare behind him and the whole area at the back of the corral exploded with angry animals. They charged through the herd, heading for the gate. In moments the entire field was filled with billowing dust, stampeding horses, and shouting cowboys. From his place

against the back rail, Niño could see only confusion and
the press of the horses trying to get out the opening in
the corral. None of the men were in sight. They had had
to move aside to make way for the thundering charge.
Part of the corral fence fell and the horses streamed
toward the gate in the wall like a flood of raging water.

And then Niño recognized his chance. He hadn't
planned it—he didn't even know what he was going to do
to take complete advantage of it. But he dug his heels into
the bay and it lunged forward. With the fluid ease of long
practice, he swung down under the horse's neck and
locked his heels over its withers. He felt as if his arms
were being pulled out of their sockets and he choked on
the thick dust that rose from all those pounding hoofs. But
he hung on.

"Close that gate! Close that gate!" It was Don
Armando's voice. "Don't let any more get out!"

Niño did not know where he was in relation to the gate,
but he heard the creaking of hinges.

"Oh, Turquoise Woman," he prayed, "help me get out!
Oh, gods, smile on me!" Then to make sure he omitted no
one, he prayed again, "Please God of the Padre, Virgin
Mary, all the saints, get me past that gate!"

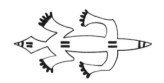

# *Chindi*

THROUGH the clouds of dust Niño caught a glimpse of the adobe walls and in seconds he was beyond them. He dropped his feet and sprang up so he was astride the bay without breaking its headlong pace.

A quick glance behind him told him he had been seen. Don Armando stood with rifle raised and pointed in his direction. Suddenly there was a scream and Niño saw Tomás in the path of some stampeding horses. He looked as if he were falling.

Niño did not pause and he had no time to feel grief for Tomás. "I am out!" he thought in wonder. "I am free!" The beat of the horse's hooves matched the singing of his heart. "No more am I Niño. Now I am Straight Arrow—and I am free!"

The stampeding horses were pounding behind him, a dark wave of frenzied animals intent on only one thing—running. Anything in their path would be trampled. Another clap of thunder only drove them faster.

He was vaguely conscious of two riders—one to his right and one on his left. They were yelling and waving their sombreros, trying to turn the herd, to get it milling.

Straight Arrow lay low on the bay's neck, while his heels drummed steadily, hoping he would not be seen.

Through the cloud of dust he recognized one of the riders—Miguel! He was yelling—a sound of pure joy—as if he found this dangerous, wildly galloping ride exciting. Miguel was ahead of him and Straight Arrow knew he posed a threat to his freedom.

Even as the thought touched Straight Arrow's mind, Miguel's saddle flew in the air—a broken cinch! He saw Miguel's arms grab the horse's neck, and he held his own breath, waiting. Miguel had done that trick of hanging under the neck only twice, and neither time had he done it too well. Then the desperate, clawing hands lost their grip and Miguel disappeared. Straight Arrow heard a scream—then silence.

The crush of the stampeding herd drove him forward until he came to where Miguel had fallen. Then gripping the horse tightly with his legs, he bent over and grabbed the blue checkered shirt, never slowing the bay. Somehow he managed to drag the bloody body up and over the animal's neck, where he clutched it to keep it from sliding off.

The stampede was heading south and he knew every rider at the hacienda would go that way to round up the horses. So he headed northeast. Even as the bay galloped over the uneven ground, putting more and more distance between him and the hacienda, Straight Arrow could hardly believe what had happened. But his earlier moment of jubilation was gone. He was not yet free, and Miguel was badly hurt.

When the bay tired, he had to stop. He slid Miguel to the ground by a mesquite, then dismounted while sending up a prayer of thanks to the gods that today he had slipped a halter on the bay. It was a thing he almost never did—but now he could tie it securely to the tree. He climbed a knoll that showed him the landscape in all directions. The wind had changed and was driving the black thunderclouds off to the west. Southward he saw a cloud of dust—large enough to mean the herd of horses. But there were no signs of any riders between himself and that dust cloud. No one was coming after him yet, which gave him a good head start.

He went back to Miguel and tried to stop the flow of blood from the many wounds. The handsome face was badly cut, a leg was broken, and it was clear he had been hurt inside.

Around Miguel's neck was the leather cord with the mouth organ. It was dented slightly on one end, but otherwise it was not damaged. He removed it and slipped the cord around his own neck, stuffing it inside his shirt. He felt so close to Jake at that moment, almost as if Jake stood beside him, hat back on the straw hair, eyes crinkled with laughter. Only Straight Arrow did not laugh. His heart was heavy—for Jake and for his dying son.

"I have no water," Straight Arrow thought in despair, and even if he had, he knew there was little he could do for Miguel. Yet he couldn't throw him over the bay and ride on—Miguel was too badly injured. But to stay meant certain recapture.

Father Sun traveled steadily westward and still Straight

Arrow did not leave. This was Jake's son, and he could not leave him like this. Had not Jake saved him from many floggings, helped him find a friend in Tomás, and made life more tolerable during these four long years? Had not Jake loved him, even as Red Band had loved him? No, for Jake's sake, he had to stay.

But even as the sun went down, so did Miguel's life ebb away. Straight Arrow moved off, filled with dread. Miguel, dead, was now *chindi*! If he, Straight Arrow, didn't want the evil spirits to curse him, he would have to flee at once.

Shivering, even though the evening was still hot, he leaped astride the bay and raced away. Then he stopped and looked behind him—every fiber of his being tense with dread. Slowly he wheeled the bay around and rode back. He did not want to do it—he would be exposing himself to every kind of evil and he would surely be caught and killed. Yet doggedly he returned, not letting himself think of what would happen.

He dismounted beside the body, and steeling himself to do it, he lifted Miguel and threw him over the bay, tying him on with Miguel's own belt. Then he sang every chant of purification he could remember, calling on all his gods to protect him, because he would be exposing himself doubly to trouble—he had touched the dead and he would be traveling at night when evil spirits roamed, searching for victims.

Slowly he began leading the bay back to the hacienda. As a Navajo, he could leave Miguel's body out on the desert. But as Jake's friend he could not do it, because

Jake would want to know what had happened. And Jake would want to have the Padre say prayers over the body and bury it in the ground. Straight Arrow had seen it done when the Mexicans died of sickness.

One by one the stars appeared, and finally, a crescent moon peeked shyly from behind a cloud. Even before Straight Arrow could see the big wall looming menacingly ahead of him, he heard the wailing and the crying. Then he remembered Tomás—was he dead, too? His heart was heavy, because Tomás had been his friend.

Slowly and silently he neared the gate, then gently he slipped Miguel's body off the bay and laid it on the ground. He touched the mouth organ under his shirt. It was not wise to keep something that belonged to a person who had died. But, he reasoned, this thing that made music was not really Miguel's. It belonged to Jake. And he wanted this one small thing that Jake had valued so much that he had given to his son. It was all Straight Arrow had now to remind him of the yellow-haired white man.

The bay whinnied and a voice somewhere behind the gate bellowed, "Who's there?" It was Francisco!

Terror-stricken, Straight Arrow leaped on the bay and thumped his heels on its sides, riding as he had never ridden before. He could not see in the darkness, and fervently he hoped the bay would not stumble in some rabbit hole.

From a distance he heard the squeaking hinges of the gate and he glanced back. A lantern moved in the blackness, and as it was lowered, a wail came drifting back to him.

He sighed in relief. Miguel had been found and he had done what had to be done. Now he was free to go home. Mile after mile he rode, and the farther he went, the more he was torn with confusion and uncertainty. He should have been overjoyed at the idea of returning to Tsegi Canyon, yet the ecstasy he'd felt upon first getting beyond the gates was gone. He felt as if he were going back simply because he'd thought about it for so many years that he couldn't think of anything else to do.

He admitted to himself that reluctance to leave Jake was part of his dilemma. But he was loath to acknowledge the other reason—the strongest one—that he was no longer a warrior and felt removed from the life of the Navajo. All these four years he had refused to give up his beliefs, his Navajo culture, staunchly holding on to his Navajo pride. Yet now he felt an outcast. Like Esteban and Felipe—he was nothing.

When finally the bay grew tired, he tied it to a tree and lay down to sleep. At the first light of dawn he started out again, dodging whenever he saw a soldier in the distance.

At midday he topped a mesa and looked back. A tiny moving puff of dust told him someone was already out searching for him. His mouth tightened. After yesterday, Don Armando would be doubly determined to capture his escaped slave—if only for the satisfaction of killing him.

Straight Arrow sought out the rockiest ground—traveling always northeast—in order to leave as little trail as possible. Whoever was after him—probably Francisco— would use up precious time looking for whatever faint trail the hard ground would yield. Staying in the cover afforded by gullies, trees, and thick brush, he rode now at a fast walk so that his own horse would not give off a dust cloud signal to anyone from the hacienda, or to a soldier.

By mid-afternoon his stomach was rumbling with hunger. He knew, too, that both he and his horse would need water, so he began looking for green foliage. When he saw a ribbon of rich green brush running along the bottom of a narrow canyon, he started the bay down the incline. At the bottom he found a stick and dug a hole about a foot deep in the sand near some graceful willows. Then he sat back and waited, alert to every sound.

It took some time for enough water to accumulate in the bottom of the hole to satisfy his thirst, but he waited patiently. Curious about the mouth organ, he pulled it from under his shirt and put it to his mouth and blew. Startled at the screeching noise, he put it away quickly and looked around, wondering if he had been heard. Then he pulled it out again, this time blowing softly. It made a sound. He went from one end to the other, blowing, as he had seen Miguel do. The sound that came out was not gay music like Miguel's, it was noise. With a sigh he stuffed it under his shirt and checked the water. The hole was nearly full. After he had drunk his fill, he let the horse drink and when they were both satisfied, he filled the hole with sand, erased as much of the evidence of his presence as possible, and rode off.

For four days Straight Arrow traveled in the same fashion, walking his horse to avoid raising dust and hiding whenever he saw soldiers, who seemed to be everywhere searching for stray Indians. He ate roots and berries and sometimes a rabbit when he was lucky enough to trap one in a snare made of sticks and a strip of cloth torn from his shirt. He knew that the gods did not look with favor on Navajos who ate raw meat. Hadn't they taught them to cook so that they would not be like the animals? But he was afraid to betray his presence with a fire, and without meat his strength would soon fail. So he ate his rabbit raw and with each bite he asked the gods to forgive him.

He made an easy crossing at the Rio Grande and smiled sadly, remembering Tomás' efforts to teach him to swim so he would not have trouble at this river. But the bay was a strong swimmer, and in any case, the river was not swollen now as it had been before.

Once across, he felt he could travel faster because he was not as afraid of being recaptured. He saw only one band of soldiers and the distant rider behind him who never seemed to come any closer or to fall any farther behind. Water became more and more of a problem. Once again he was grateful for Red Band's training. He was even glad that life at the hacienda had not been easy and that he had had to work many afternoons in the hot sun with no water to drink until dusk. In its way, those four years had been training for survival, too—different from Red Band's, but training nonetheless.

On the fifth day, Straight Arrow saw a horseman on the ridge ahead of him, riding south. He hid his bay near a spring some distance from the trail, then went back to wait for the rider to pass. Before he came into view, Straight Arrow heard singing. To his amazement, he recognized a Navajo chant. He grinned with joy as the

man came down the path on a sorry-looking paint horse—a
Navajo clad in deerskins and moccasins and wearing a big
silver concho belt and a necklace of turquoise. He had a
pinched face that looked out of place above his broad
shoulders.

As he came closer, Straight Arrow stepped out from his
hiding place and greeted him.

The man stopped. "I am surprised to see you here, my
brother," he said. "I thought the soldiers had removed all
the Indians from this area." He smiled suddenly, exposing
black and broken teeth. "But I am glad to see that it is
not true. I am called Dark Feather and I ride south to
search for my sister's daughter who was stolen four winters
ago."

"What would her age be?" Straight Arrow asked,
although he knew of no other Navajo children in captivity.

"She would be now about your age."

Suddenly he remembered the girl who had been in
Manuel's cart with him. "I know of only one girl that
age—she had a broken tooth. . . ."

"But that is the one!" Dark Feather exclaimed. He
dismounted and Straight Arrow saw that he was short and
squat. "Tell me—where can I find Broken Tooth? Is she
well?"

Straight Arrow shrugged and explained where he had
seen her. "I have no way of knowing where she might be
now," he ended apologetically. "I have myself just escaped
from slavery."

Dark Feather clicked his tongue. "These are sad times,"

he said. "But who are you and where are you going now?"

Straight Arrow hesitated. How strange, he thought, that a Navajo would ask such personal questions. "I am called Straight Arrow and I go to Tsegi Canyon," he answered finally. "But I ride in fear of the soldiers. I see you do not, since you sing as you travel and do not bother to hide your trail."

Dark Feather pulled a paper from a pocket in his shirt. "This gives me permission to search for Broken Tooth and tells the soldiers not to stop me."

Straight Arrow glanced at the paper and thought about how fast he could travel himself if he didn't have to worry about being stopped by the soldiers. He looked up at the sky. "Soon Father Sun will go to sleep. You are welcome to share my meat and my camp for the night."

"I have eaten nothing for the last two days and my belly rumbles with hunger," Dark Feather said.

"Come then. I have my horse hidden at a spring not far from here."

Dark Feather smiled. "You are clever," he said as he followed Straight Arrow from the trail.

When Straight Arrow produced his rabbit meat, Dark Feather insisted on building a small fire so they could cook it. "Do not worry," he said confidently. "No one will bother us as long as I have the paper." He patted his pocket.

"But I have no such paper, and I do not want to go back to the hacienda."

"Do not worry, I tell you," Dark Feather said again,

fanning his fire vigorously. "Trust me. There are no soldiers near here right now. But if one should come, I will say that you are my brother."

Something warned Straight Arrow that this man was treating the whole affair of the soldiers too lightly. And how could he know there were no soldiers around? If that piece of paper were so powerful, Straight Arrow decided he must somehow get it for himself.

While he ate the roasted rabbit meat and the ample supply of roots they were able to find, his uneasiness returned and this time he realized that it sprang from distrust of Dark Feather. He said he was hungry, but he did not eat like a hungry man. And why should he have been without food for two days when he knew very well how to find roots?

"Were you at Bosque Redondo?" Straight Arrow forced himself to ask this one personal question.

"Yes—but I have been back home for some time now."

"My mother was there—Slender Woman of the Bitter Water clan."

Dark Feather shrugged. "There were so many of us. . . ."

Dark Feather seemed reluctant to talk further of Bosque Redondo or even of Broken Tooth and his search for her. Straight Arrow's suspicions grew stronger. He began to think that this man had never even heard of Broken Tooth until he himself had mentioned her. He remembered now that the girl's tooth had looked newly broken, as if she had been struck when she was captured. If that were the case, she would not have been called Broken Tooth when her uncle knew her.

Straight Arrow was ashamed of his suspicions, but he could not quiet them. This was the first Navajo he had seen in four years. He wanted to accept him, but there was something about Dark Feather that he did not like. Before they had finished their meal, Straight Arrow made up his mind to leave quietly when Dark Feather slept, even if he had to go without the paper. In the meantime, he would be watchful.

After he had eaten, Dark Feather removed his deerskin shirt and threw it over a rock. "I will refresh myself and water my horse at the spring," he said as he walked away.

Straight Arrow waited until he heard the horse sucking water, then he darted to the shirt, snatched the paper out of the pocket and ran to the place where his bay was tethered. He would not wait for Dark Feather to sleep—he would ride now.

"It is not wise for a Navajo to ride at night," Dark Feather said, stepping out from behind a bush. He grinned maliciously as he pinned Straight Arrow's arms to his sides. There was a quick twist of rope, and once more Straight Arrow was a prisoner!

"Why are you tying me?" he demanded.

"So that I can more easily deliver you to the soldiers." Dark Feather took the paper from Straight Arrow's hands and stuffed it in his waistband.

"For stealing your paper?" Straight Arrow was truly amazed. Stealing was not a crime to a Navajo.

Dark Feather shoved him toward camp. "No—not for that. I put it there so you would steal it. I wanted your attention fixed on something like that to help make my job easier."

"What job?"

"Capturing Indians and taking them to the soldiers. They pay me."

Straight Arrow could not believe his ears. One Navajo selling another to the white men? "You would betray your own people!"

"Why not?" Dark Feather pushed him to the ground and bound his ankles. "We will wait here. In another day or so the soldiers will come by and I will turn you over to them. It is very easy and it pays well."

"You—you coyote!"

Dark Feather shrugged. "Go to sleep. I do not want to hear you. I am tired."

Straight Arrow lay awake all night. His brain was as numb as his arms from shock. He could neither sleep nor think, but lay in a hopeless stupor, knowing that he was doomed—whatever happened. Because prison would mean death from despair, as surely as a return to Don Armando would mean death from a bullet.

The bitterest thing of all was that this had come upon him through one of his own people and when he was on his way home. Home!

"Turquoise Woman, have you forsaken me?" he groaned. And he was not surprised when there was no answer. Had he not ignored the *chindi*?

# The Stranger on the Trail

ALL the next day Straight Arrow waited, sick and helpless. He was so tightly bound that there was no way he could get loose. Near the end of the day he made one more feeble effort to shame Dark Feather into letting him go. "What do you get when you sell one of your own people to the white soldiers? What would make such a betrayal worthwhile?"

"A bag with twelve pieces of silver and your horse, which by the way, is a fine one, much better than mine."

There was a long silence, then Dark Feather continued, his voice bitter. "You think it terrible what I do," he said and grunted in scorn. "This is what the white man drives us to do. I was once a warrior—I killed many Utes, many Mexicans—before Bosque Redondo. But now among our people there are· no warriors—only foolish men who behave like women." He spit into the fire. "I cannot hoe the fields, tend the sheep, cut the wood. That is for others. It is not for a warrior such as I." His head rose haughtily. "I would rather do this. I get money. Someday I shall go back to my people, but I will have many horses then, much money, many sheep. I will let others do the small work. I will be important." His black eyes flashed in fury, as if by his words he would defy them all.

Stunned by this angry tirade, Straight Arrow could only stare at him. Yet beneath his astonishment was a flicker of compassion, because the man's thinking mirrored his own doubts that had troubled him for days, slowing his travel homeward. He had thought to go back to be a warrior and have his people sing his praises, as they had done to his father.

But was this what he was going back to—the life of a sheepherder, doing the work of women? Would he be like New Found Boy instead of like Red Band? He could not accept such a thought. To behave thus would be no better than being a slave on Don Armando's hacienda.

That night, in sheer exhaustion, he slept while Dark Feather snored some distance away. The fire had died out and he opened his eyes to total blackness when he was wakened suddenly by a hand clamped hard over his mouth. He could feel a knife cutting his bonds, but he couldn't see who was doing it.

"Come," a voice whispered softly close to his ear. It was Jake!

Straight Arrow rubbed his wrists and ankles, trying to restore circulation. When he was able to move normally, he inched away from the camp, then followed the shady form ahead of him until they reached the horses. Jake murmured assurances and moved his hands over their bodies to silence their nervous pawing.

"You take the paint," Jake whispered as he swung up on the bay. While Straight Arrow was still mounting, he

moved off, then they both dug their heels into the horses'
sides and charged ahead. As they crashed through the
darkness, they heard Dark Feather yell in outraged
surprise. Straight Arrow laughed aloud—without a horse
Dark Feather couldn't even follow them!

"Let's get over where I've got my buckskin tucked out
of sight, Niño," Jake said when they were a safe distance
from the camp.

"I will no longer be called Niño," the boy replied. "I
am Straight Arrow. . . ."

"Straight Arrow, son of Red Band," Jake said softly, as if
feeling the words. "Now that's a right fine name for you,
young'un. But you mustn't get your back up if I forget
once in a while. . . ."

Straight Arrow laughed as they jogged through the
night. "If you forget, I will not answer, because there is
no more Niño."

They picked up Jake's buckskin and Straight Arrow once
more mounted his bay.

"I reckon we'll make tracks north," Jake said as they
started out. "Isn't that where your canyon is?"

"Yes."

"Thought maybe I could ride with you, since we're
going the same way."

The sadness in Jake's voice surprised Straight Arrow,
though he knew it shouldn't have. After all, Jake had just
seen his only son die in a terrible way. But for the past
few days escape had been the only thing on Straight
Arrow's mind, and though he had missed Jake, he had
given little thought to what Jake would do. Now he

realized Jake faced another big change in his life. For all of the years of Miguel's life, he had lived at the hacienda, as much a prisoner as Niño, himself. Only it wasn't ropes, floggings, or an adobe wall that kept him working for a man he despised; it was love for a golden-eyed boy who had been given a chance to grow up as a fine *caballero* instead of a "shabby cowboy." Now Jake was free to go wherever he wanted. But the sadness in his voice told Straight Arrow that Jake would have gladly traded his freedom to be a captive at the hacienda again, teaching and guiding his son, tempering Don Armando's arrogance and cruelty with his own love and gentleness.

His own heart overflowed with love for this simple man. "Straight Arrow welcomes his friend, Jake," he said quietly.

They picked their way carefully through the darkness, leading the bony old paint. "I had you in my sights a dozen times," Jake told Straight Arrow after they'd traveled a long distance, "but I couldn't catch up to you. Figured you thought somebody was hunting you down, and you were up to your old Indian tricks to throw me off the trail." Jake chuckled softly in the darkness. "When I saw your campfire last night, I decided you thought you were safe, so I kept out of sight. And this morning I watched your camp through my field glasses to see who rode out. When I saw no one, I got curious and decided to poke around after dark." He paused. "Good thing I did."

"Yes," Straight Arrow said with heartfelt satisfaction.

Then he added indignantly. "Do you know what that
coyote does? He sells his own people to the soldiers—a
Navajo. . . ."

"Navajos—whites—there's snakes and coyotes in all tribes
and races, young'un. And there's some as trusty as a
cowpoke's best mount."

Straight Arrow snorted. "There are no good Mexicans."

"No?" Jake sounded amused. "Well, let's see now—how
about Consuela?"

"All right then—Consuela." Straight Arrow grinned in
the dark.

"And Tomás, young'un—how about him?"

Ashamed that he had not thought to inquire about
Tomás until he was reminded now by Jake, he asked,
"Tomás—was he hurt when he fell?"

"Shucks, you taught that boy to ride. You ought to
know he's most nearly as good as you are at tricks."

"You—you mean he did that deliberately?"

"Yep. He saw his pa draw a bead on you, so he acted
like he was falling. Before Don Armando caught on to
what Tomás was doing, you were out of range."

"Did Don Armando—was he very angry with Tomás?"

Jake sighed. "No, young'un, he didn't have time to be
angry. Y'see, we all saw Mike. . . ." His voice broke and
he was silent as they rode side by side. When he could
speak normally, he added in a low voice, "That was a fine
thing you did, Ni—young'un, rescuing Mike like that—you
two not being good friends and all—a real fine thing."

Straight Arrow wanted to add, "But *you* are my friend

and that is why I did it." Yet he couldn't say it without telling Jake he knew the story about Miguel. If Jake wanted him to know, he would tell.

Jake said nothing, however, and they rode silently. Straight Arrow wanted to talk, or chant, to drive away any evil spirits hovering about in the blackness. But Jake's heart was heavy, he knew, and the deep occasional sighs told him Jake's thoughts were back at the hacienda with a son he would see only in memories now.

They rode until well after dawn, then stopped to rest in a small canyon. Jake rummaged around in his bedroll and pulled something out, throwing it quickly to Straight Arrow. It was his blanket!

"Figured it'd be cold crossing these mountains and you'd need it." Jake seemed embarrassed. "Go on, now, roll yourself up and get some shut-eye. We've got to get moving again soon."

For the next three days Jake kept a close watch on all horizons with his field glasses so that they were able to avoid the small groups of soldiers. They moved swiftly northward, eating rabbit meat and sage hen, yucca root and wild potatoes. The weather grew sharp at night but the days were never more than pleasantly cool.

As they sat around their campfires after dinner, Straight Arrow told Jake of his life in Tsegi Canyon, ending with his own capture by the Ute and being sold into slavery. But he said nothing about his uneasiness in returning home now. In fact, during the past few days he'd been so content with Jake's company that he had almost forgotten his concern.

Jake, in turn, told of his adventures as a young boy, leaving a place called Ohio and crossing the wide grassy plains, the high snow-covered mountains, and ending up in the hot desert country. Then a search for adventure led him to Mexico.

Straight Arrow could picture the fun-loving, yellow-haired young man, his blue eyes bright with the life of excitement, his face creased as he laughed, riding around Mexico with all the skill of the best *vaquero*. No wonder a young girl like Catarina forgot she was of noble birth and fell in love with this laughing cowboy who played gay music.

But Jake's stories always ended when he worked as a *vaquero*—never when he became the overseer at the hacienda of Don Ramon. And he never spoke of Miguel. If Jake suspected that he, Straight Arrow, had brought Miguel's body back because of love for Jake, or because of love for Tomás, Straight Arrow did not know. It would take time, he knew, before Jake would be able to talk of Miguel to anyone—time to let the memory of him grow dim. Only now, after so long a time, had Straight Arrow been able to speak about his own family.

Straight Arrow found that as the time for him to part from Jake approached, he dreaded the thought of their separation. He knew now that Jake had come with him to keep him out of the hands of the soldiers and to see him safely home. He felt a love for him that was stronger than his instinctive distrust of all white men.

Then the day came when they stood together at the edge of a wide, deep canyon. Steep red sandstone walls rose majestic and, sheer from its flat and sandy bottom. One slender column soared almost a thousand feet from the canyon floor.

Unable to speak, and fighting hard to keep his face impassive, Straight Arrow stood overwhelmed with awe and joy at the first sight of his beloved canyon.

Finally he said in a voice that broke in spite of all his efforts to control it, "That—that is Spider Rock." He swallowed hard. "This is Tsegi Canyon—my home!"

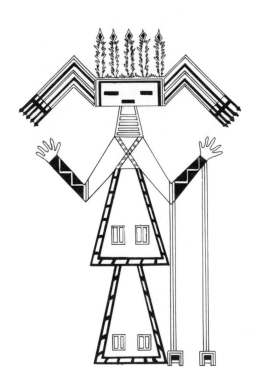

# In Tsegi Canyon

"THAT'S a mighty pretty word—home," Jake said slowly. "And it reminds me, I'd better be getting along to make one of my own somewhere, now that you're safely back."

Straight Arrow said nothing. He should be anxious to get going, yet he looked down at the tiny hogan visible near where his own had once stood, and he felt reluctant to go on. Two figures worked in a cornfield, but they were too far below for him to tell who they might be. But with sinking heart he recognized one as a man!

He glanced at Jake helplessly, then back to the canyon. To go down there and find his family meant becoming a farmer, a sheepherder—living a life as miserable as the one he'd just left.

"You know, young'un," Jake said in a voice tight with suppressed emotion. "It's going to seem odd not having you around. I've kinda got used to you." He cleared his throat while he pushed up his hat and scratched his head. "I'm hankering to buy a ranch of my own—saved a fair pile of money—and I thought maybe. . . ." He looked at

181

Straight Arrow then stared down into the canyon. "Well, y'know, maybe your folks never got back, and you've got no home to go back to. And there's not much call for warriors nowadays, so—well, shucks, kid, I'd sure like to have you ride along with me. You could be my waddy—my head honcho with the horses—sort of boss of the ranch next to me." He looked back, his bright blue eyes sad, despite the half smile on his face. "I always hankered to have a son run the ranch with me. Can't think of anyone who could fill the job better."

Desperately fighting to hide his feelings, Straight Arrow looked down at his horse, his strong brown fingers nervously toying with the bridle. Had Jake recognized his reluctance to go back to an existence void of the excitement of the warrior life? Certainly what Jake offered was more appealing. He loved Jake almost as much as he had loved Red Band, and it was hard to imagine life without him now. He also loved horses. With Jake he would have many horses—and he would be Jake's son— important as Miguel and Tomás had been important at the hacienda. And his family was probably dead, anyway. Hadn't Jake said over half of them had not lived through the ordeal of Bosque Redondo? And even if they were alive, by now they considered him dead. They would not miss him.

Every fiber of his being longed to go with Jake. Yet his glance returned to the tiny figures on the canyon floor. He was a Navajo, and this was where he belonged—digging in cornfields if necessary.

"In my heart I shall always feel as your son," he said in

a low voice, looking straight ahead because he could not look at Jake and still keep his face impassive. "But I am a Navajo. Even if my family is dead, I must help my people."

Then, to ease the disquiet within himself, he smiled and looked at Jake, speaking in a lighter tone. "But come with me into my canyon. If my family lives, I would like them to know the white man who has shown me kindness. If they are . . ." he stiffened, unable to voice the thought that they would be dead, then he went on in the same light voice, "in any case, I would like you to see my homeland."

Jake snorted. "I'd just as soon ride into a stampeding herd as to go in there, young'un!"

"Why?"

"After what you Indians have been through at the hands of the whites, I'd be about as welcome as a rattlesnake in a bedroll."

"But it was the soldiers who made us suffer—and you're not a soldier. You are my friend."

There was a long silence. Finally Jake nodded. "All right, I'll go with you to see your folks. And if they didn't come back—you can come along with me."

Straight Arrow shook his head. "For me there is no other place."

That night, still on the rim of the canyon, Straight Arrow lay looking up at the black, star-studded sky. It was different from the sky anywhere else, he thought—clearer, closer, because it looked down on the sacred land of the Navajo. The desert night was full of sweet smells and he

thought that nowhere else had the air been so fragrant or
so crisp.

He took the turquoise out of the knot in his headband,
and sat up, holding it close to the fire. "Someday I'll make
a silver bracelet," he told Jake, "and put this blue stone in
it. I will wear it to remind me that it was from the
moment I put it into my headband that I knew I would
one day come home."

Jake shook his head. "I reckon it was you, more than
that hunk of blue stone, that got you here. You were the
most determined kid I ever saw. You just wouldn't
knuckle under to anybody."

"But the turquoise made it possible," Straight Arrow
insisted. "This one and the other that Tomás gave me."
He dug into his pocket and brought it out. "You have
never seen it."

Jake whistled. "Whoo-ee—that's a beauty."

They fell silent then, and Straight Arrow thought about
his family. Maybe he wasn't a great warrior now, but at
least he was not returning empty-handed after fours years
away. He had his two pieces of turquoise and two horses.
And he would be able to show Slender Woman where
their silver and turquoise were hidden. With that, they
could buy sheep, so New Found Boy could have flocks to
tend.

The next morning they came around to the wide flat
entrance of the canyon. Straight Arrow saw Jake hesitate,
then reach into his bedroll and draw out a gun. He
slipped it into his waistband, hidden under his shirt, and

gave Straight Arrow a sheepish grin. "Just in case," he murmured.

Soon the canyon began to narrow and its red walls curved up and away against the dazzling blue sweep of the sky. The great cottonwoods that lined the winding river shone gold in the morning sun. Crisp red-brown leaves clung to the white branches of the sycamores and rustled gently as the breeze moved among them. To Straight Arrow it seemed as if the whole world had put on a blaze of color to welcome him home.

They had not gone far into the canyon when they came upon a man hoeing a field. His hair in its *chonga* knot was streaked with gray and his face was as thin as a hatchet blade. When he stood up to watch them approach, he was bent and stiff.

"Do you make a new home here?" Straight Arrow inquired after the proper period of silence that Navajos always observed when meeting.

"This has always been my home," the man answered shortly. "But the white soldiers destroyed it." His eyes were flat black as he looked at Jake.

"My friend is not a soldier," Straight Arrow hastened to explain. "We have traveled many days together and he has helped me to come safely home." He returned to the subject of the land. "If this was your home, you must be of the family of Brown Shirt."

"I *am* Brown Shirt." The man's eyes lost their flatness and there was a remembering in them. "I was a warrior then—before the soldiers came—and I had horses and sheep. I had a hogan here and a. . . ." He focused again on the present and spat in the sand. "Now I have nothing. And I am called, not Brown Shirt as before, but Bent One." He spat again, close to Jake's buckskin this time. "Take your friend and be gone."

"It is hard to believe," Straight Arrow murmured as they rode on. "He was a man younger than my father. Now he looks like Grandfather." A new thought struck him. "He did not know me, yet I played there often with his sons."

"You've changed, too, young'un, don't forget. Why didn't you tell him who you were?"

"Word that I've returned might reach my mother before I do—if she is here." He was more shaken than he wanted to show by his encounter with Brown Shirt. It had never occurred to him that his family might have changed so much that he would not know them. And seeing the great warrior so old and bent, now hoeing fields like a woman, was a terrible shock. What was there to live for?

They pressed deeper and deeper into the canyon and he saw Jake tense as the walls rose higher and steeper around them. Every family they passed was busy rebuilding hogans and corrals and clearing ravaged fields. From what they told him, all of them had lost at least one member of the family to the long disaster at Bosque Redondo. Dread of what had happened to his own family grew stronger, the more Navajos they passed.

Straight Arrow saw a few scrawny, carefully-tended sheep and goats and only three bony horses. He saw the young men eye his bay and Jake's buckskin—and even the sorry paint—with longing.

It was mid-afternoon when Straight Arrow once more saw Spider Rock in the distance. His heart pounded in a strange mixture of expectation and dread. Soon he would know whether his own family had survived. And he hoped. And was afraid.

As he rounded a narrow bend in the canyon, he heard the plaintive bleat of a lamb that had evidently become separated from its mother. He dropped from the bay to lift the lamb and toss it over the horse's back. As he remounted, an arrow whizzed by him so closely that it tore the sleeve of his cotton shirt. It was then that he saw a slender young Navajo watching him from a cleft between two boulders. His face was hard and threatening and he had a second arrow ready to go.

"I come in peace," Straight Arrow called out quickly.

"Then return that lamb," the young man ordered.

"I was only taking it to its mother."

"Put it down."

Straight Arrow dismounted and put the lamb back on the ground. He looked at Jake who sat motionless on the buckskin with both hands in view on the horn of his saddle.

Straight Arrow walked toward the Indian. He felt that he knew him, yet he couldn't quite remember who he was. His broad, flat face with its full lips compressed into a tight line was familiar—but no name came to mind.

"I seek a family who lived here before Bosque Redondo," Straight Arrow said.

"There is no one beyond Spider Rock except my family, and I am Gray Fox. Am I the one you seek?"

"It is the family of Slender Woman I want to see."

"Why?" The one word was at once a question and a challenge.

"She is my mother."

The hardness vanished and frank curiosity took its place. "Who are you?"

"I am called Straight Arrow."

Gray Fox shook his head. "No," he replied, "Straight Arrow is dead." He raised his bow and arrow once again. "I do not know what you want with Slender Woman, but I will not let you distress her with such a story."

"But I *am* Straight Arrow. . . ." It was a cry that burst from his heart. His mother was alive! "I was captured and sold as a slave—I am Straight Arrow, I tell you!"

Once more the weapon dropped as Gray Fox stared first at Straight Arrow then at Jake. Satisfied finally, he said in a low voice, "Then you are my brother. . . ."

Straight Arrow gasped. "*You* are New Found Boy?"

"I was once called that," Gray Fox admitted. Then he smiled and his whole face changed. The hardness melted and the gentleness Straight Arrow knew so well looked out from his shining black eyes. He leaped from his place on the rock.

Straight Arrow was hardly an inch taller than his brother as he clasped his hand in the firm Navajo grip. "My brother," he said.

Gray Fox looked at him closely. "Yes, I can see now that you are Straight Arrow." There was a trace of bitterness in his voice. "I think that we have all changed. You are welcome, my brother. It will warm the heart of our mother to see you alive and well. She has mourned you as dead." He turned from Straight Arrow to Jake. "But why do you bring a white man here?"

"He is my friend."

"I cannot think of any white man as friend." His voice was hard, as he stared at Jake, then he shrugged. "If he befriends you—he is welcome. Does he speak our tongue?"

"No—Spanish or English, but not Navajo."

Gray Fox nodded to Jake. "You are welcome here," he said stiffly. Then he turned to his brother with that gentle smile. "Let us go to the hogan of our mother."

"I bring back two horses and some turquoise," Straight Arrow told his brother as he mounted his horse. "We will buy sheep for you to tend and I will once more be the hunter for our family."

Gray Fox did not reply. He refused Straight Arrow's offer of the paint and moved easily beside them on foot.

"Who's your friend?" Jake asked as they rode past Spider Rock.

"He is my brother."

Jake's eyebrow rose. "Your brother! Well, if that don't beat all. I always heard Indians never showed emotion, but this! If I'd just seen my brother after all those years, I'd be pumping his arm and slapping his back and maybe even hugging him, I'd be so tickled to see him."

Straight Arrow smiled. "That is not the Navajo way. But I think I am just as glad to see my brother as you would be to see yours."

Straight Arrow was impatient to get to his mother, but he held his horse to a slow walk so that his brother could keep up. As they approached the new hogan which stood

near the wall not far from the one he remembered, he
saw a slight figure rise stiffly from its bent position in the
garden plot. Even at this distance he knew it was his
mother by the pounding of his heart and the tightness in
his throat. And suddenly he could wait no longer. He
loped out ahead of the others, leaving the paint for Gray
Fox to bring in.

He dismounted and strode to the woman in the field.
Her hair—black as night in his memory—was now almost
entirely gray. Wisps of it had escaped from its severe knot
and straggled across her lined face. It warmed his heart to
see her still in the traditional dress of the Navajo
women—two long panels of handwoven cloth, secured at
each shoulder and tied about the waist with a piece of
frayed rope. Once it would have been a silver belt—and it
would be again, he vowed.

His mother knew him at once—he saw the recognition in
her eyes. She made no move to embrace him, but grasped
him tightly by his arms with hands that were calloused
and swollen. When she raised her eyes to his face, they
were wet with tears.

"I thought you dead, my son," she murmured brokenly.

Straight Arrow knew she yearned to take him in her
arms, but she would never disgrace her warrior son by
such weak behavior. For his part, he longed to tell her
how many times he had thought of her—how much he had
missed her, but this would not do either. So he merely
said, "I saw my father killed, then I was taken captive. I
have been a slave."

She released him as Jake and Gray Fox came near.

"This is my friend, Jake," Straight Arrow told her.

His mother addressed Jake directly in Spanish. "You are welcome, friend of my son. Come into our hogan and rest. I will prepare food for you." She turned to Gray Fox. "You will come, too. We have much to talk about."

Gray Fox shook his head. "To visit would be pleasant, but to lose a goat or sheep would bring us hard times. When it is dark and all is safe for the night, then I will hear the stories of my brother." His warm smile included them all as he turned and walked away.

When they went into the hogan, Straight Arrow was pleased to see that he had grown so much he had to stoop in order to get through the low doorway.

Without even thinking, he went to the west wall of the round room where the men always sat. Jake followed him and they both dropped crosslegged onto the dirt floor. As Straight Arrow's eyes grew accustomed to the dim light, he saw Grandfather huddled asleep against the wall beside him. He was wrinkled almost beyond recognition, his hair was white and his mouth was pleated loosely around toothless gums. Slender Woman roused him enough to tell him the good news. He nodded agreeably and seemed to go back to sleep.

"Where is Timid One?" Straight Arrow asked.

There was an eruption of blankets and Grandfather spoke. "She drowned in the big river with an old woman. They let them both drown, those white devil soldiers—on the way to Bosque Redondo. Your mother was so distressed that she was sick—the baby came too early. . . ."

With aching heart Straight Arrow remembered the Mexicans beside the Rio Grande who had told of such a drowning. "I saw it from a distance," he said. Now he would never see Timid One again, nor ever know the baby that had come too soon.

Slender Woman was warming a stew of squirrel meat, roots, beans, and wild onions for them. Its fragrance filled the hogan and made Grandfather chomp his toothless gums greedily.

"You eat well," Straight Arrow commented.

Slender Woman agreed. "The animals have had four years to multiply without being hunted. There is an abundance of small game."

"I will ride up on the rim and bring you something big," Straight Arrow boasted. "Deer—or cougar—so that we will have plenty."

Slender Woman smiled into her fire. "That will be good, my son."

Straight Arrow took the bowl of food, remembering his dreams—never being able to taste his mother's stew. He put some in his mouth, savoring the onions and the rich gravy, feeling the chunks of meat on his tongue. Then, blissfully, he swallowed it.

While they ate, Slender Woman told about their four years of hardship. There was never enough food and Straight Arrow realized it had been as Jake said—every time the Indian had planted seed, their crops were destroyed by floods or too salty river water, or grasshoppers.

"The soldiers gave us a white powder to eat," Grandfather broke in when he had cleaned his plate. "Who among us had ever seen such a thing? We did not know what to do with it but we were so hungry we would have tried anything." He shook his white head and looked accusingly at Jake. "I saw three small children eat it dry. They choked to death. They died in my arms fighting for breath. The white men are devils!"

Straight Arrow knew Jake didn't understand Grandfather's words, but there was no mistaking his feelings. His hate hung in the room like an evil spirit.

"He is old and angry," Straight Arrow mumbled, embarrassed for his Grandfather.

"The white powder was flour," Slender Woman took up the tale hastily. "Later we learned from the soldiers how to mix water, baking powder and salt with it to make a dough we could fry." While they helped themselves to more stew, she continued. "The white men also gave us hard beans that never softened no matter how long we boiled them. It was a long time before we learned to boil the beans then throw them out and drink the water. It is a thing called coffee."

Grandfather was still thinking about the flour. "Even that powder was scarce and filled with bugs that made us sick." He leaned toward Jake, his faded eyes burning with hate. "You stole our land and gave us nothing to take its place. We could no longer hunt to feed ourselves, so you let us starve and die of disease." He reached across Straight Arrow and shook a bony, twisted finger under Jake's nose. "You call us cruel—oh, I've heard you—but it

is you who are the cruel ones. You killed the husband of
my daughter. You killed half our tribe at Bosque Redondo!
Think of it—thousands of my people are dead—because of
you." His old body trembled as he stretched out both
hands toward Jake's throat.

Jake shrank back against the wall.

"My father!" Slender Woman cried. "He did not do
these things—he is not our enemy."

"His skin is white," the old man said flatly as he sank
back into his blankets.

"Forgive him, please," Slender Woman said to Jake.
"He is old and he is confused from all his suffering. . . ."

Jake nodded, but his glance went to the doorway as if
he were judging the distance in case he had to get out in
a hurry.

Grandfather continued to mumble and mutter about the
misery of their captivity while Slender Woman and
Straight Arrow looked at each other helplessly. Good
manners forbade their interrupting an elder while he
spoke. But finally his anger spent itself and, exhausted, he
lay down—a crumpled pile of bones inside his blanket—and
slept.

"It is true that life was not easy at Bosque Redondo,"
Slender Woman said. "But not all the soldiers were bad.
Some even tried to help us though they had little enough
food to eat themselves. It was the government that was
evil. They did not send enough food, enough blankets.
They did not plan places for us to live. Grandfather
remembers only that and forgets that anyone was ever
kind." She stirred the small fire.

"Your brother learned to steal food," she said proudly, "and the soldiers could never catch him. That is when he earned his new name, Gray Fox. In the deep snow he went with the men to hunt deer, although he was yet a boy. Many came back with nothing. But never Gray Fox. We would have died had it not been for the cunning and skill of your brother. . . ."

Forgetting his manners, Straight Arrow broke in. "If I had been with you, I would have taken care of you even better. And I would not have let Timid One drown. . . ."

His mother looked at him strangely before she went on with her story. "When we walked back from Bosque Redondo—starving, ragged, and sick—your brother kept us fed and hopeful. He found a goat that was nearly dead and nursed it back to health. From this we got milk and still do to this day. When we got home he stole a fine goat from Fort Defiance. Again at a later time he was gone for two days and returned with a ewe which soon gave birth to a lamb." She smiled with pride. "Thus we have survived and thus we prosper. With the two sheep promised to us by the government, we will have the beginnings of a small herd and someday we will again have a large flock. Gray Fox will see to it."

Straight Arrow said nothing because he was not sure what he wanted to say. He was glad that his mother and Grandfather and Gray Fox were safely home. And he knew that for four years he had had no thought in his mind but to return to his home and family so that he could protect them. Now that he was here, he knew he should be happy and satisfied.

But something was wrong. He looked at Jake seated uneasily in the hogan and knew how he felt. For some strange reason, Straight Arrow felt he didn't belong here either.

# *Home*

WHEN the meal was finished, Slender Woman returned to her cornfield and Straight Arrow took Jake to see where he and Red Band had climbed the ladder and to show him the canyon where they had hidden. But he could not bring himself to go into the eastern canyon where Red Band had died. To him that canyon would always be *chindi,* where not only the evil spirits dwelled, but where his own heart had known its greatest loss.

Then while Grandfather slept and the others were busy, Straight Arrow climbed the talus slope of Spider Rock. With a stick he dug for the buried treasures and was rewarded shortly by a glimpse of sheepskin. He clawed away the rest of the dirt and lifted the bundle. The contents spilled out on his knees—Red Band's big concho belt, the small belts that had belonged to him and to New Found Boy, Slender Woman's turquoise. . . .

He touched the silver discs of Red Band's belt and felt so close to his father that he could almost hear his voice and see the approval in his eyes. Joy welled up inside him, but he hid it with a frown. It was not good to let the gods see him too happy.

He ran all the way home and hid the precious bundle under his sheepskin. Then after the evening meal, he laid it beside the fire in their midst. The silver—dull now from disuse—gleamed in the firelight and the turquoise shone green-blue against it. The family exclaimed with joy and he felt satisfied.

"You have brought us great happiness," Slender Woman said. "We had thought our turquoise lost forever."

Grandfather got to his feet and fastened his belt around his waist. While they all watched, it slowly slipped down over his hips and legs and fell to the ground. Grandfather looked at them and laughed. "Mine is too big and yours is too small, my grandson. Maybe we need to exchange."

Straight Arrow laughed, hardly able to contain his excitement at the plan he would tell them. "With this we can buy many sheep and many horses," he said with shining eyes. "We will be poor no longer."

There was a momentary pause. "Yes, it has many uses, my son," Slender Woman finally said in her gentle manner.

A fury Straight Arrow could not understand made it hard for his face to remain passive. He had found their turquoise and silver for them and told them of his plans to use it, and all they could do was act as if he were discussing something as unimportant as the food they ate!

"Their years at Bosque Redondo have dulled them," he thought irritably and was once again grateful for Red Band's training that had kept him sharp in his wits throughout his slavery. So deep was he in the memories of

what he had endured that his mother's next words shocked
him.

"I think we should use our turquoise and our silver to
have an *Enemy Way*."

Grandfather clapped his hands in approval and Gray Fox
looked pleased. Only Straight Arrow sat in stunned
silence. He had forgotten about the *Enemy Way*. It was a
very special ceremonial performed whenever warriors
returned from their battles. It was intended to cleanse
them of the evil spirits that had come from exposure to
the enemy, the dead, or to other harmful things. It was
chanting and games, and a symbolic killing of all foreign
influences.

"We have wanted to have an *Enemy Way* for Gray Fox
ever since we came back and rebuilt our hogan," Slender
Woman continued. "But we had nothing to pay the *hatalis*
and nothing to trade for food. Now that you are home, my
son, it is even more important to have a sing. We will
wash away all the evil influences of the white men." She
glanced guiltily at Jake sitting apart, looking ill at ease
among these strangers, then as if remembering that he
could not understand Navajo, she continued. "We will
have a big sing—everyone will come."

Straight Arrow said nothing. In spite of his efforts to
hide his joy this afternoon at Spider Rock, the gods must
have seen! An *Enemy Way* lasted three days and was very
expensive, for the family of Slender Woman would have to
feed everyone who came. It would be a disgrace to have
the sing and not feed people generously—especially since

most of the Navajos were suffering from lack of supplies now. Also it would be wrong not to pay the *hatalis* handsomely. But what a waste of the silver and turquoise that could buy so many sheep and horses! He saw his dreams of wealth disappear.

Gray Fox was looking at the jewelry uncertainly. "I think there is not quite enough," he said. "It has been so long since our people have had a sing in the canyon. Everyone will come. The cost will be great—especially if we must buy cornmeal and not flour. And we must build a special hogan for the ceremony—it is the custom."

Straight Arrow clutched the large piece of turquoise in his pocket. Almost against his will, his hand drew it out.

"I have here one more piece," he said reluctantly. "The stone given to me by my friend, Tomás. Take it."

Slender Woman looked at him, her eyes soft with love. "Your friend's gift will make our *Enemy Way* possible," she said.

The voices of Slender Woman and Gray Fox droned on as they talked of the plans for the *Enemy Way*, but Straight Arrow scarcely heard them. His own thoughts were in confusion. He was home. It was the fulfillment of a desire held in his heart for four miserable years. Yet life was not as it had once been. He had not expected it to be so, but neither had he expected to feel a stranger here.

There could be only one answer—the others had changed. Certainly Gray Fox was not as Straight Arrow had known him. He remembered how he had once recognized a quiet strength in the small boy, but nothing in that gentle guardian of the herds had prepared him for the young man who sat beside him now—a hunter, warrior, and savior of his people. What had brought the change?

The answer, when it came, was very simple. It was the same thing that had made Straight Arrow brave enough to bear cold and hunger and beating and humiliation without a whimper. It was the same thing that had given him the courage and the strength to remain a Navajo in the face of all the Mexican attempts to change him. It was love and respect for Red Band and for the way of the Navajo.

How then, Straight Arrow asked himself, could he resent what his brother had done?

Restless, he got up and strode outside, pacing up and down in the darkness by the hogan. "You taught us well, my father, better than any of us knew," he thought in sudden humility, "and because of that your family lives and is together once more."

With this humility came another realization—as clear as if Red Band had spoken the words aloud. Somehow in spite of all his efforts, he had returned to his people with ways that were not Navajo!

It was true. Perhaps he had thought he could shed the "enemy ways" with his cotton shirt and other Mexican trappings. But it was not so. The list of his shortcomings passed before him.

He stared up at the stars, the same stars he had watched so many times at the hacienda, and in memory he was back there, seeing himself as he was.

He had been jealous of his brother when Slender Woman had praised him—the way Lucia had been jealous of Tomás.

He had thought himself better than others, because he was the warrior son of Red Band—even as Miguel had strutted like a jaybird because he thought he was a nobleman.

He had looked on the turquoise of the family as his own—something *he* could decide to barter for sheep and horses—as Don Armando might have done. "But not as you would have done, my father," he murmured.

He had come home wanting to be received as a hero. And when he had learned that his own suffering was nothing beside that of Slender Woman, Gray Fox, and Grandfather, he had sulked like a small child. Like Lucia when Tomás proved himself a horseman. Like Don Armando when his son did not ride out to welcome him.

Straight Arrow bowed his head in shame as he thought of Gray Fox. It was not his brother who needed the *Enemy Way*. It was himself.

Then all pain was swept away in a flood of gratitude to Slender Woman and to Gray Fox. They, too, knew all that the turquoise would buy in sheep and horses. But there was something of greater importance to them than wealth—the *Enemy Way* for him, so that he could be at peace in his home.

He raised his head again, his face smiling as he looked up at the heavens, and a sweet calm spread through him. Now he wanted that *Enemy Way*. He had seen the evil

spirits in himself, and soon the ceremony would drive
them out.

He stepped into the hogan again, feeling at peace with
himself, and his eyes met Jake's. Their glances held for a
moment, then he looked away, smiling faintly. How wise
this white man was—almost as wise as Red Band.

Jake had known of the Niño ways in Straight Arrow's
thoughts, and he had known that Straight Arrow would
not be happy in his home. So he had offered to take him
away and give him a feeling of importance. But Jake had
seen the Niño routed out of him tonight.

A sadness dulled the edge of Straight Arrow's peace—
tomorrow Jake would be gone. His reason for coming into
the canyon was wiped away, and he would be anxious to
begin his new life somewhere.

Slender Woman rose, giving her son a smile of
understanding. "It is time to sleep," she said as she
banked the fire for the night. "We are all weary with this
long day."

The family unrolled their sheepskins inside the hogan,
but Jake insisted on sleeping out of doors. Straight Arrow
did not argue. He knew Jake was concerned about
Grandfather and would sleep better if he were outside
where he had more room to maneuver if it became
necessary.

The next morning Grandfather shuffled out of the hogan
to begin the sunrise chant and they all followed him. To
Straight Arrow's suprise, the old man showed consider-
able strength, standing as erect as his bent back would

permit and raising his arms to the Father Sun. Gone was the wavery voice and trembling body. It was Grandfather more as Straight Arrow had known him before.

Breathlessly Straight Arrow watched as the sunlight touched the tip of one wall, then another. It glanced into a side canyon, rested on an outcropping of red rock, and slipped across the highest branches of a golden tree.

As the chant ended, he took a deep hungry breath of the crisp autumn air and felt his heart burst with love for this land. A sudden breeze shook the branches of the cottonwood beside the hogan and the leaves came down around him in a shower of light. He caught one in his hand. He had seen many such leaves at the hacienda, he thought, but none as bright or shining gold as this.

As soon as the morning meal was ended, Jake saddled his buckskin. "Reckon it's about time I got to hunting a place of my own," he said. He bid farewell to Slender Woman and Gray Fox and smiled in understanding when Grandfather turned and shuffled away without speaking.

Slender Woman looked up at him shyly. "The friend of my son will always be welcome in our hogan."

Jake cleared his throat. "He's been like another son to me. . . ." Abruptly he mounted the horse and turned away.

Straight Arrow jumped on his bay. "Wait, I will ride with you to Spider Rock."

They rode together then, for the last time in silence. Jake's words, "He's been like another son to me . . ." repeated themselves over and over in Straight Arrow's thoughts. He wanted to tell Jake that even as Jake had learned to love him like a son—as he had also loved his "Mike"—so had Straight Arrow learned to love him as a father. Red Band had taught him what he needed to know to survive in the world of warriors. But Jake had taught him how to live in the world of peace with others. But such words would not come.

When they reached Spider Rock, Straight Arrow took off the blue headband and untied the knot. "I give this to my friend," he said as he put the small turquoise into Jake's big palm.

"I can't take your last piece of turquoise, young'un."

"I will find more. Take it, and may Turquoise Woman protect you as she has me, and help you find your home."

Jake put the stone in his pocket.

Straight Arrow reached under his shirt and lifted the cord from around his neck and placed the mouth organ in Jake's hand. "It is said to make gay music, but I cannot do it," he said huskily. "It is for you to play."

Jake sucked in his breath in surprise, then their glances met—Straight Arrow trying to keep his face impassive and knowing he had failed, and Jake's eyes misting over. No words were needed. Jake knew! Jake knew why Straight Arrow had risked his own freedom to bring Miguel's body back to the gate. And that knowing, Straight Arrow felt deep inside his own heart, had somehow wiped away a loneliness in Jake.

"A son to be proud of," Jake whispered and turned his horse. Without looking back, he headed for the mouth of the canyon.

Straight Arrow watched until he was out of sight. Then

he lifted his eyes to the graceful red column that reached like a finger into the clear blue sky. The soldiers had done their worst. They had killed and pillaged, they had tricked and humiliated the Navajos and stripped them of all that they held dear. But in four long miserable years, they had been unable to destroy them. His people had returned to their sacred land hungry and poor and miserable—but they *had* returned, because they were the *Dineh*—the unconquerable People, and this was their home.

And he was still a warrior. Maybe he could not go on raids and fight the Utes, the Apaches, or even the white soldiers, as his father had done. Instead, he would provide for his family and wrest a living from this barren land. That's what Red Band had taught him—taught them all—not just to fight, but more important, to survive.

Suddenly a strange, lilting music drifted back to him—music at once gay, yet sad. He smiled. Yes, Jake would find his home somewhere. Did he not have gifts from his two sons—turquoise for protection and music for happiness?

With a light heart, Straight Arrow turned his horse and headed for home.

## About The Author

LYNN GESSNER was born in Cuba of American parents, grew up in Central America, and settled with her husband in the American Southwest. She draws on a deep knowledge and love of these lands and their effects upon their inhabitants for her moving novel, *Navajo Slave*. Life at a trading post during her teen years inspired the author to a thorough study of the Navajo Indians. When not pursuing her love of traveling, Mrs. Gessner makes her home in Scottsdale, Arizona.